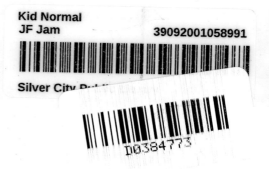

KID
NORMAL

KID
NORMAL

GREG JAMES & CHRIS SMITH

ILLUSTRATED BY
ERICA SALCEDO

BLOOMSBURY
CHILDREN'S BOOKS
NEW YORK   LONDON   OXFORD   NEW DELHI   SYDNEY

BLOOMSBURY CHILDREN'S BOOKS
Bloomsbury Publishing Inc., part of Bloomsbury Publishing Plc
1385 Broadway, New York, NY 10018

BLOOMSBURY, BLOOMSBURY CHILDREN'S BOOKS, and the Diana logo
are trademarks of Bloomsbury Publishing Plc

First published in Great Britain in July 2017 by Bloomsbury Publishing Plc
Published in the United States of America in June 2018
by Bloomsbury Children's Books

Library of Congress Cataloging-in-Publication Data
available upon request
ISBN 978-1-68119-709-8 (hardcover) • ISBN 978-1-68119-953-5 (e-book)

Book design by Andrea Kearney
Typeset by RefineCatch Limited, Bungay, Suffolk
Printed and bound in the U.S.A. by Berryville Graphics Inc., Berryville, Virginia
2 4 6 8 10 9 7 5 3 1

To find out more about our authors and books visit www.bloomsbury.com
and sign up for our newsletters.

To LJ

—Chris

To Kid Normals everywhere.

Always say yes to an adventure

—Greg

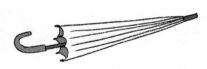

KID
NORMAL

1

The New House

Murph hated the new house more than he could remember hating anything, ever. A light wind, such as you often find at the beginning of a story, tousled his shaggy brown hair as he stood looking up at it. He was trying to work out, with all the power of his just-eleven-year-old brain, why it made him feel so incredibly rotten.

The problem with the new house was . . . it was just so *new.* When Murph was smaller he'd lived in a much older house, with interesting wooden stairs that led to an interestingly dingy attic full of interesting boxes, and there was a garden with interesting trees to climb and interesting tree houses to build. It had been the sort of house adventures happen in—although, to be fair, they never actually had. But the *potential* was there.

Now there was no chance those adventures would

ever happen. Four years ago, Murph, his mom, and his brother had left that house behind when his mom's job had forced them all to move to a new town. That had been bad enough. But, just a year later, they'd had to move again. And then again. Then again. So here he was, a third of his lifetime away from the rambling old rooms he'd loved so much, staring at yet another new house and wishing someone would blow it up or set it on fire. Which, in fact, they would. But he didn't know that just yet.

Even if Murph had known that the new house would be a smoking ruin within a few short months, it wouldn't have cheered him up very much. Underneath a brownish drizzly evening sky that matched his mood perfectly, he heaved cardboard boxes into the boxlike house and dumped them in the echoing hall, which was painted a pale shade of green almost exactly matching the color of cat vomit.

Murph's new bedroom was painted a different but equally horrible green color, an out-of-fashion avocado. It was a prime candidate for the Most Depressing Room in the Awful New House Award, and it was up against some stiff competition. It had nothing in it except a mattress on the floor and a white dresser. Had it been daytime, the curtainless window would have offered a view of the oily canal at the back of the house and a brick wall on the other side. Murph was glad it was dark.

With a sigh, he unzipped his bag and started to unpack, chucking jeans and T-shirts into the drawers more or less at random. Eventually he came to the last four items in the bag, but instead of putting them away, Murph laid them out on the bare mattress and sat down cross-legged on the floor to look at them.

They were four gray shirts—the shirts he'd worn on his last day at his last four schools. The first was covered with signatures in marker: it had been a tradition there that if someone was leaving, everyone got to write a farewell message.

We'll miss you, buddy, from Max
Stay in touch, superstar! Sam
Don't leave us, Mighty Murph! Lucas

There were other signatures and messages, too, covering most of the gray material with cheerful, multi-colored letters.

Don't leave us!

But he'd had to leave—all because of his mom's job. And he'd meant to stay in touch—but he'd been busy that following year, making new friends to replace the ones he'd had to abandon.

He picked up the second shirt and read the names of those new friends. Not so many names on this second shirt, but still some kind words.

Can't believe you're moving after just a year! Love, Pia

Murph! We'll miss you. Come back soon, bud. Tom

Shirt number three had only a couple of names written in pen as a last-minute thought; he'd wanted some kind of memory to cling onto.

The fourth shirt was clean and unmarked.

Murph folded the shirts back up and piled them into the bottom drawer of the white dresser.

He'd made no friends in the last year. He'd been convinced, and rightly so, that one day soon his mom would break it to him over dinner that they were going to have to move again. Other people had become like TV shows to Murph. There was no point getting too involved, because you never knew when someone was going to come along and change the channel.

As you'll know if you've ever moved, the First Night Takeout is a very important ritual. And like every family that's ever moved into a new home, Murph; his brother, Andy; and his mom sat down to eat takeout that night with a weird feeling that they were in someone else's home, and someone really needed to turn up the heat.

They ate out of the aluminum foil containers because his mom couldn't find the box with the plates in it. Murph knew exactly which one it was, but he was too busy stopping his older brother from stealing his spring rolls.

"Those are mine, you big lump!" he shouted as Andy reached across like a greedy octopus and pulled out a greasy roll.

"You don't need a whole bag to yourself, Smurph Face!" the big sixteen-year-old lump replied.

"Yes, I do," spluttered Murph, food debris fountaining out of his mouth like the end of one of those big impressive fireworks, only greasier. "And don't call me Smurph Face. You know I don't like it."

"Sorry, Smurph Face," said Andy proudly, with the air of someone who'd just said something incredibly clever.

"Come on, you two," sighed their mom. "Andy, don't call your brother Smurph Face. And, Smurph Face, share your spring rolls."

"MOM!" shouted Smurph Fa—sorry—*Murph*. The others chuckled, and he reluctantly joined in. "You're

ganging up on me. As if it wasn't bad enough getting dragged to nowheresville to live in a shoebox. I am not a shoe!"

His mom put a comforting hand on his cheek. "I know you're not a shoe. And I know you didn't want to move again." Murph watched as she tilted her head back, apparently to fend off a couple of mom-style tears. *She didn't want to come and live here either*, he thought to himself.

"I know it's going to take a while to settle in," Murph's mom told them both, "but just you wait, boys. You'll have a great time in the end, I promise. We're going to make the best of things here. It's going to be . . ." She paused, searching for the right word, and though Murph didn't realize it at the time, she found the perfect one. "It's going to be . . . *super.*"

2

A Misunderstanding

There were a lot of things Murph and his family didn't know about the new town. But the most important thing they didn't know was where Murph was going to go to school. His mom had tried to figure it out before they arrived, but everywhere seemed to be full, and as the hot days of August drew on, she became more and more obsessed with finding him a spot.

She spent all evening on her laptop, chatting to other parents and trying to get tips. She even started accosting random moms and dads in the town and asking them where their children went to school, and whether any of their friends were leaving the country. Murph was mortified. Andy, who was five years older and had a place at a local high school, thought it was hilarious. "Maybe you can teach yourself at home," he teased him. "We'll get you a few books and you can set a timer telling you when you can take a break."

Murph didn't think that was funny at the time—and he thought it was even less funny when August rolled into September and Andy went off to high school. "Still no school for you, little bro, sorry," he said, ruffling Murph's hair as he headed out the door.

It was just about the worst week so far. Murph tagged after his mom as she went for meetings at every junior high school in town. Curious faces watched him as he tailed her past packed classrooms and into the offices of different headmasters. He sat quietly and, as instructed, tried to look unusually clever. But every time the answer was the same: they would just have to wait.

Then, a few days into this head-meltingly depressing process, Murph and his mom were on their way home from shopping. The streets were fairly empty; most people were inside having their dinner. A woman and a boy only a little older than Murph turned out of a dingy-looking side street not far ahead, and they overheard her saying, "So, how was school?"

Murph's mom, whose ears had developed a bat-like ability to home in on any word connected to education, sped up, gripping Murph's hand tightly.

"Mooooom, let go!" he pleaded. But looking up at her face he realized there was no point arguing—this was Mom on a mission.

By the time they'd crossed the road, the other boy and his mother had already climbed into a car. For a moment Murph was worried his mom was going to spread-eagle herself on the hood to try and stop them from leaving. But instead, she turned into the side road they'd come out of, still dragging Murph along behind her like a low-quality kite.

If the street had looked dingy from a distance, close up it was positively murky. A few cars were parked on the scrubby grass, and the lawns in front of many of the grubby terraced houses were so scruffy, it looked like the garbage cans were actually there to nicen them up a bit.

But about halfway down the street was a large school. They knew it was a school because, apart from the railings and familiar-looking classroom buildings on the other side of the front yard, there was a metal sign over the gates that simply read:

THE SCHOOL

A man was in front of it with his back to them, locking the gates.

Murph actually heard a loud clicking sound as his mom gritted her teeth with determination and began to cross the road.

"Clean yourself up," she hissed at him so fiercely that he actually did try and iron the front of his T-shirt with his hands. Then she changed her tone completely and fluted "Excuse me!" in a voice that would have put even an unusually fancy duchess to shame.

The man slowly turned around.

Murph's mom had started to say "Excuse me" again, but it turned into a kind of throat-clearing noise as it came out.

He didn't look like a normal sort of teacher. He had very dark, shiny, slicked-down hair with one large curl plastered in the middle of his forehead. He was wearing a shabby-looking tweed jacket, but above the elbow patches his arms bulged with muscle. Behind thick-rimmed black glasses, his eyes were bright blue. His jaw was so chiseled it looked like it had been carved out of marble.

"May I help you with something, ma'am?" asked the strange sort of teacher.

Murph's mom finally recovered her voice and asked, "This is a school, isn't it?"

The man looked very much as if he'd like to say no, but then glanced up at the sign over his head.

"Yeeeees," he replied very slowly and not very encouragingly.

"Oh, wonderful! You see, we've just moved here and I'm having terrible difficulty finding a school for my son," she began, draping an arm around Murph, "and—"

The man cut her off.

"I'm terribly sorry, ma'am; we're not going to be able to help you here. We're . . . we're not accepting applications from the . . ."—he seemed to be searching for the right word—"from the . . . the . . . we're not accepting *any* children at the moment. I'm so sorry."

There followed a moment of silence, and Murph was sure his mom was about to give up. But suddenly she grabbed the teacher by his upper arm. She needed both hands to do it.

"Please," she breathed, "*please* see what you can do. Murph's such a capable boy—he needs somewhere like your wonderful school to take him in."

"I'm sorry," said the man again, gently extracting his huge bicep from her grasp. "Good evening to you." And he began to walk away.

"He's a boy with so much potential!" shouted Murph's mom after him. "With your help he could really . . . you could really help him *fly!*"

The man stopped dead, and turned around.

"Fly?" he asked in a low voice.

"Yes, *fly.* I really think that at the right school he . . . he could," she finished rather lamely.

"So, you've just moved to the area. And your son is . . . *capable*, you say?" continued the man in a low voice.

Murph's mom nodded enthusiastically.

"And is Murph, ah, *flying* already?" he asked, dropping his voice still further and glancing up and down the road.

"Oh yes, he's been doing so well," she replied, also lowering her voice to match his. "He really wouldn't let you down."

"He's actually flying?" the man whispered.

The questioning was getting a little weird now, as well as difficult to hear. Murph was busily occupying himself with how he could get the ground to open up and swallow him. He'd seen some of his test results and it was a bit of a stretch to describe his performance so far as flying.

But his mom seemed to smell victory. "He is, he really is."

"Mr. Drench, would you come over here for a moment?" called the man softly, and another, smaller figure Murph hadn't noticed before came scurrying across the road. He was shorter and thinner than the other teacher, and had sharp, darting eyes behind round glasses.

"Flying already, is he?" he asked in a nasal voice as he walked up to them, although Murph wondered how on earth he could have possibly heard them talking.

"This is my sideki—er, that is to say—my assistant, Mr. Drench," explained the first man. "He'll take your details." He turned to Murph and held out a hand. When Murph took it, it felt like his own hand was being slowly crushed by tractor wheels. "Murph, we'll see you on Monday. I look forward to seeing how you get on with that flying." He swooshed around as if he was wearing a cape, but then swooshed back again: "And obviously don't, er, *tell* anyone about The School, will you?"

"What, we can't tell anyone? Because it's a secret school?" Murph's mom laughed at her own joke.

The two men looked confused for a moment, and then, nervously, the hugely muscled man began to laugh as well. "Ha ha, yes, of course I don't need to tell you. Silly of me."

The smaller man looked between them in confusion as they continued chuckling. Murph just smiled nervously and wished he was invisible.

Murph's mom and the unusual teacher laughed for slightly longer than necessary. Then an awkward silence fell.

"So, is it secret, then?" she asked with a nervous grin.

"Oh yes," replied the man, swirling around once again. "Until Monday, then," he called over his shoulder as he marched away.

Murph and his mom caught each other's eye in total bemusement. Then she shrugged and turned to Mr. Drench, who had pulled a stack of forms from one of his pockets.

3

Mombarrassment

Murph had a tingling feeling in his stomach.

It had started mid-morning on Saturday and had grown steadily throughout Saturday night. When he woke up on Sunday morning it felt like there was a fairly large collection of baby eels migrating through his insides. And by Sunday evening he couldn't sit still without feeling sick with worry, so he paced up and down in the new house's tiny backyard.

His brother had been no help at all. When they had relayed the weird "secret school" conversation to him, he'd found it hilarious.

"Ooh, do you have to get on a magical steam train at a hidden platform?" he'd hooted as he ran up the stairs after Murph, who was trying to escape to his room. "Will you have to go to a special shop to choose a wand?"

"Shut *up*," hissed Murph between gritted teeth, closing the door on Andy's foot and trying to keep it shut with his shoulder.

A muffled cry of "Hope you're not hiding an owl in there!" could be heard as Murph finally managed to lock his door and collapsed onto his bed.

Andy had enjoyed the joke right through the weekend. But now it was Monday morning, and Murph's mom had woken him up so early that he felt as if he should be shaking a few birds awake on his way down to breakfast. Andy was old enough to get the bus to his school on his own, so he was still lounging in bed, listening to the radio.

Murph's sleepy stomach was in no mood for toast, and his sleepy hair was in no mood to be brushed, but nevertheless, by the time most of us are just about thinking of having a really good morning pee, Murph was already being hustled toward the car.

You see, Murph was one of those kids who have to get dropped off ridiculously early. His mom's shift at the hospital started at eight o'clock, a long drive away across town. It had always been the same. For years now his weekdays had started with hanging around school alone like a knowledge-hungry ghost.

Actually, Murph had come to enjoy seeing the inner workings of it all, before the kids came and broke the silence. He liked watching the milk get delivered; he enjoyed chatting with the janitors; he liked seeing his teachers arrive in various states of readiness for school. It was like being backstage at a theater before the curtain went up, the only difference being that once the play finally got going, there was no one to sell ice cream during the intermission.

Murph would have loved an ice cream at 11 a.m.

But we're getting distracted.

"Go on, then," Murph's mom encouraged him as she pulled up outside The School. She leaned over and opened his door. "Be brave!"

Murph gave her a resigned look, swung his bag over his shoulder, and jumped out of the car.

As his mom drove off around the corner she beeped the car horn. This is classic mom embarrassment or, to use the technical term, *mombarrassment*.

Other acts of mombarrassment include:

- Kissing you goodbye in front of your friends
- Calling you by your baby nickname in front of your friends (Murph's was "Honeyhugs." When his mom had used it in public two schools ago, he'd actually been glad he was about to move again)
- Telling you to "stop showing off" in front of your friends
- Asking if you have a girlfriend/boyfriend in front of your friends
- Asking if you have a girlfriend/boyfriend in front of the girl/boy you want to be your girlfriend/boyfriend
- Singing loudly in public
- Cleaning your face by licking a finger
- Asking if you have a handkerchief, as if you were a fancy lady from the olden days

After what seemed to be the world's longest beep, Murph threw his mom a half smile, half please-stop-beeping face, waved meekly, and hefted his bag onto his shoulder to begin what was to become the single most bizarre day of his life so far.

The school gates were open, but there didn't seem to be anybody around. Murph wandered across the yard and through the open front doors, calling out "Hello?" in a tiny first-day-at-school voice. But there was no reply.

Just inside, Murph found a scratched wooden desk with an ancient-looking computer on top. He decided to settle down on the uncomfortable plastic chair behind the desk to wait for whatever happened next.

At Murph's last school there had always been plenty of activity as the first bell loomed closer. Parents chatting, kids rushing around, cars double-parking or getting chased out of the drop-off zone by the unusually fierce crossing guard. But here everything seemed to be much quieter. He watched kids walking calmly across to the gates, and spotted a dad dropping his daughter off in a very sleek black car. Two much older boys sauntered past him, and he thought they must have smuggled a firework in, because there was a loud bang just as they rounded the corner.

"Nice Cape, Howard!" he heard one of them say, and they both laughed.

Neither of them was wearing a cape, but that still didn't make it funny as far as Murph was concerned.

The only thing that seemed different for a while was that everyone seemed to be heading into school rather quickly and quietly. It was all very organized, even without a crazy crossing guard to keep things in order.

But as the start of the school day drew nearer, things did begin to cross the line into weird. In fact, they leaped way over the line and came closer to "What the cheese and pickle salad is going on here?"

While he waited for someone to come and tell him what to do, Murph gazed out the window. It was a gray, rainy day, but suddenly, a bright yellow figure underneath an umbrella appeared out of the low-hanging clouds and drifted rapidly down and out of sight behind one of the school buildings.

Murph couldn't believe his eyes. Was he tired? Was he hallucinating? Was he going mad?

Maybe it was a giant canary, he thought.

He quickly rationalized this idea away, remembering that giant canaries aren't a thing (but wishing briefly that they were), and then tried to work out what had just happened. He had to find out what this lemon-colored thing was.

He got up from his desk and dashed out, following the trajectory of the giant canary—or the thing that couldn't possibly be a giant canary, not least because of the umbrella. He turned to the left, traced the direction of the figure in the sky, and raced toward the fields.

Next to a side door marked **Coatroom**, he saw a yellow figure flicking water off its arms and doing that openy-shutty thing that has no name, that you use to make umbrellas dry.

In fact, let's give that thing a name right now. From a short list of three—**flofting, blatting**, and **flumphing**—we have selected the word **flumphing**, and we hope you like it.

The figure was **flumphing** an umbrella vigorously.

Murph approached quickly as the figure glided into the coatroom. Just as the door was closing, he twisted his body to try and slip inside unnoticed. But instead he

skidded on the wet floor, careered inside like an ice-skating rhino, and collided with a damp yellow wall.

As he scrambled to his feet, he was relieved—mostly—to find that the figure he'd seen flumphing the yellow umbrella wasn't a giant canary but a very normal-looking, bespectacled girl.

"Sorry! Hello! Um, did you, fly . . . sorry, canary . . . boots . . . massive bird, it's raining . . ."

Murph was panicking. He wasn't great with girls at

the best of times, let alone when they had, quite literally, just floated into his life.

"Hello, clumsy," replied the girl, calmly taking off her glasses and doing that grown-up polishing thing on the end of her obviously yellow woolen scarf. "I'm Mary. Who are you?"

Murph was so shocked that an apparently occasionally airborne girl was making conversation with him that he momentarily forgot his own name.

"Mar— . . . Murph."

"Well, Mar-Murph, lovely to meet you. Are you a new student too?"

This was the moment for a really world-class comeback.

"Yes," Mar-Murph replied sheepishly.

"Okay, well, help me off with this coat and I'll show you to our classroom," commanded Mary.

Again, this seemed to Murph like a great cue for a devastatingly funny line. A real zinger.

"Okay," he said, helping umbrella canary girl gather up her belongings while approximately twenty-seven immediate questions buzzed unhelpfully around his head.

Murph picked out one of those questions as they zipped through the hallways. He thought he'd go for the big one first: "Um, Mary . . . did you just come to school, you know . . . through the, er, through the actual air?"

"Yep," replied Mary, like it was the most normal thing in the world, "but let's keep that between us two, shall we? I don't think I'm really supposed to. But it's quicker than walking, and I was late."

"Okay, cool, just checking," replied Murph breezily, trying desperately not to freak out. "Also . . ." Murph had another question. "Are you called Mary because of Mary Poppins?"

"Who?" replied Mary, looking confused.

"Oh, nothing. Just thought, y'know, because of the umbrella sky thing . . . ," burbled Murph.

"What *are* you burbling on about?" said Mary, raising her eyebrows at him so they rose over the rims of her glasses like two hairy blond suns. "Right, here we are. Follow me. This is Mr. Flash's classroom."

"Mr. . . . *Flash*?" Murph just had time to say before she bundled him through the door.

4

CT

To begin with, Murph was relieved to find that everything inside the classroom looked more or less normal. Two teachers were standing at the front of a class of kids all noisily settling into chairs and dumping their bags under desks. One was the chiseled-chinned teacher he'd met at the school gates. He greeted Murph with a very hearty "Ah, good morning to our new arrival!" and began moving toward him, holding out an upraised palm as if introducing a minor celebrity.

Mary looked impressed. "How do you know Mr. Souperman?" she asked Murph.

"Mr. . . . Super*what*?"

Mary shot him another one of her looks. She did looks. "Boy, you really *are* new, aren't you? Mr. Souperman's the headmaster. I'll save you a seat." She whisked off.

It was becoming apparent to Murph that Mary was taking him under her wing, even though she didn't have any wings.

Murph grinned up at the headmaster in a bemused way.

"Morning, Mr., er, Souperman."

"Ready to get started with that flying?" He beamed.

Murph nodded politely back at the big friendly face, although midway through the second nod, his eyes widened slightly as a thought occurred to him. He glanced over at Mary. *Flying . . .?*

His brief thought was rudely interrupted.

"Right, then," Mr. Souperman said, striding to the door. "Mr. Flash will get you going."

Mr. Flash? thought Murph again as he scuffed his sneakers over to the desk next to Mary and sat down. *Sounds more like something you scrub the bath with than a teacher.*

Like the headmaster, Mr. Flash seemed to have been spending some time in the gym. Like, weeks at a time. His upper arms bulged as if his shirtsleeves had been stuffed with cuts of roast pork. His head was bald and extremely shiny, and his mouth was almost entirely obscured by a droopy red mustache. He was wearing army fatigues tucked into tall black boots.

As the before-class commotion continued he raised his chin so that he was looking down his nose at everyone. **"SHUUUUUUUUT UP, THEN!"** he barked. Gradually the shuffling and chatting came to a stop and the class regarded him in silence. His left muscle seemed to ripple slightly of its own accord. He

abruptly turned his back and began to scribble on an old-fashioned blackboard, talking as he did so.

"My name, for the benefit of our new arrival," he said, squeaking the chalk with a noise like a gerbil being squashed, "is Mr. Flash. And welcome"—*squeak*, *squeak*—"to your first lesson today."

The list of things that confused Murph about his new school was growing all the time. He could now add the fact that they still had blackboards, as if it were the twentieth century. But the list was about to get much, much longer.

MEANWHILE . . .

"Every story," declared Nektar, "needs a villain." He attempted a dastardly laugh but it came out a little too high-pitched, so he quickly turned it into a cough.

Nektar was dressed completely in yellow and black. His boots were bright yellow, his pants jet black. Above a yellow belt, he was sporting a black shirt topped with a yellow vest. His head was almost completely covered by a black helmet with bulging yellow eyepieces and topped with two quivering antennae. Basically, if you're not getting the picture yet, he had really gone for a theme.

He was in a mean mood. Wasps usually are.

Anyway, more about him in a minute. Don't forget him, will you? The big guy who's half wasp.

Right, back to Murph . . .

Forty minutes into Mr. Flash's lesson, Murph sat at the back of the class feeling as though his brain had been removed, played with by a kitten for ten minutes, then gently replaced. He sat with his mouth open and his brow furrowed, trying desperately to work out what was going on.

At his previous schools, classes had had names like English, math, or PE. Mr. Flash's class was called CT, but for the life of him Murph couldn't work out what it stood for. At first he went through the obvious options, like Computer Technology—but there were no computers involved. Then as things got odder, he wildly thought that it could stand for anything. Cheese Toppling? Cat Tickling? Clown Trolling?

As far as Murph could work out, it seemed to be some sort of bizarre role-playing exercise, and he could only assume he'd missed something vital in the first few weeks of the year. But he'd missed school before and usually had no problems catching up with the odd times table or creative writing assignment about what he'd done over Spring Break. This lesson made him feel like he'd been to outer space for break and landed on a totally different planet.

It started off with a boy with red hair and cheeks standing up in front of the class and striking a pose with his hands on his hips. Mr. Flash looked at him approvingly: clearly this guy was a star student.

"Right, Timothy," beamed Mr. Flash, "let's see how you're progressing, shall we?"

Timothy began to strain as if he were trying very hard, but failing, to use the toilet. Beads of sweat broke out on his oversized forehead, his ruddy cheeks becoming maroon.

Mr. Flash gestured toward an old-fashioned gray TV set that was standing in the corner of the room.

"Concentrate now, Timothy," he growled. "Focus on the impact point."

"*Impact point?*" Murph mouthed, turning to Mary and giving her a quizzical stare. He'd expected her to look as baffled as he felt, but instead she gave him another cool raise of those eyebrows and a jerk of her head in the direction of Timothy.

But before Murph could turn back, there was a loud fizzing noise and a sharp flash of light. When he did look forward, there was a thin stream of smoke rising from the back of the old TV and Timothy, who was now almost entirely beet-red, was looking rather pleased with himself.

"Well, it's a start," said Mr. Flash. "Well done. But please do continue to use the remote when you're at home for the time being. We don't want another letter from your parents, do we?" Some of Timothy's friends in the front row giggled at this, and one of them tapped him on the shoulder as he sat down, as if to say "nice one."

Murph wondered what he'd just missed. Clearly the red-faced boy had done something to the TV, but how? And what? And why wasn't he in trouble? Murph had once hit a TV at his old school with a badly aimed sneaker that he'd been trying to throw to a friend, and he didn't get a "well done." In fact, he'd had to go around and wipe down all the other TVs to apologize.

But there was no time to ponder this further. Mr. Flash was ordering someone else to the front of the class.

It was the girl who'd been sitting on the other side of Mary. She had long dark hair with green ends that straggled over her face. Her sweater was baggy and her jeans were ripped. Mr. Flash didn't look quite as enthusiastic this time.

"Right. Morning, Nellie," he said in a resigned tone of voice.

Nellie didn't speak. She stood at the front of the class staring at the ground and shuffling her dirty white sneakers.

"Tell us about your Cape, then, Nellie," coaxed Mr. Flash.

She's not wearing a cape, thought Murph. Actually, Nellie was dressed as if all her usual clothes were in the wash.

She didn't respond to Mr. Flash's question.

Murph thought he heard her let out a small squeak, but it was hard to tell, because at that moment there was a rumble of thunder from outside. A sudden gust of wind opened one of the windows and sent a pile of paper flying. Mr. Flash marched over and slammed the window closed.

"Very nice, Nellie, thank you," he said.

She gets thanked for looking at her toes and not saying anything? This was even weirder than that time at Murph's previous school when Gavin Honeybun had brought in his mom's old mop for show-and-tell and pretended it was a horse.

"Great Cape from Timothy this morning, I think you'll all agree," Mr. Flash was saying. "Progressing very nicely indeed. Nellie . . . well, she gave it a try, didn't she? Now, what about hearing from the newest member of the class? Murph, is it?"

Murph shuddered into action like an old tractor. His legs lifted him into an upright position, even though he didn't recall asking them to extend. Before he knew what was going on, he was facing the class, who were looking at him expectantly. Everyone except Nellie, who was still staring at the floor.

"Now, mind the fans," cautioned Mr. Flash, pointing up to the ceiling where a couple of plastic fans were rotating slowly. "Don't want sliced boy, do we?"

He winked at Murph.

Murph stared back at him blankly. Mr. Flash might as well have been speaking French. A horrible suspicion was growing at the back of Murph's mind like unwanted mushrooms, a suspicion that he was very much at the wrong school. He had no idea what he was expected to do. In fact, he was half expecting to wake up and discover that the whole thing had been a weird dream brought on by a huge cheese overdose the night before. Murph loved midnight cheesery.

"Clear a space," warned Mr. Flash, and the front row

scraped their chairs backward, looking excited. "Come on, then, Mr. Cooper. Show us your Cape. We haven't got all day."

Why do people keep saying "cape"? thought Murph. Was this some kind of mime workshop? Would he have to pretend to be a flower growing from a seed next? He was just about to have a stab at miming wearing a cape—which we'd all have loved to have seen—but unfortunately, that very second, the bell rang.

"Ah, saved by the bell, eh?" said Mr. Flash, looking at Murph with one eyebrow raised. "Well, you'll be first up in CT tomorrow, so don't think you're off the hook. Maybe get some practice in tonight, eh? In secret, of course—I'm sure you know the rules."

By now the class were grabbing their bags and heading for the door. Murph turned on his heel and went with them, with his brain fizzing like the still-smoking TV in the corner.

5

Kid Normal

As Murph leaned up against the hallway wall, enjoying the feel of the cool paint against his befuddled brain, he felt a sharp poke in his back. It was Mary.

"Not the most impressive of starts, was it?" she asked him, screwing up the corner of her mouth.

"Well, it's a bit hard to be impressive when you've got absolutely no idea what's going on," Murph blurted out. "What on earth did I miss over the last few weeks? Was that . . . role-play? I hate all that stuff. We had a woman come into my old school and spend the afternoon making us pretend to be the farm animal we feel closest to. I was a goat."

Mary glanced at his hair and nodded sagely. "Yeah, I would have said goat. Or sheep. Your eyes are quite far apart," she said.

"Thanks a lot. Anyway," said Murph, "you've got to help me out." Behind Mary an old man, who seemed to be some sort of janitor, was pushing the broken TV on a cart. Murph gestured at it. "What was that all about? What does CT stand for?"

"'Capability Training,' of course," replied Mary, moving to one side to let the janitor pass. "You know, when you show everyone how you're getting on with your Cape."

"What is this obsession with capes around here? That's, like, the fourth time today I've heard someone talk about them, and I haven't seen a single person wearing one."

"Wearing a cape? What do you think this is, Halloween school? Not the capes you wear. Capes you *have*. You know—your Capability. What is yours anyway? By the sound of it you're like me, but without the umbrella."

"Like you?"

"Yes, you know, you're a skimmer, right? Or do you prefer the official name? 'Terrain circumvention.'"

"Now you're just making sounds, and I have no idea what they are," said Murph, resting his forehead against the wall again. "Just humor me for a minute. When you

39

say 'Capability,' do you mean, like, a skill? Because I'm pretty good at *Minecraft*—will that do?"

Mary laughed sarcastically. Then, when she saw the worried look on Murph's face, she took on a puzzled expression herself.

"Your Capability is your power, Murph."

"What, like a . . . superpower?"

"Well, nobody's called it that for, like, thirty years. But yeah, if you want to go retro"—she adopted a fake movie-trailer voice—"a superpower. You saw Timothy, didn't you?"

"Um, yeah. So what's his power . . . sorry, his Cape? Is he the Amazing Red-Faced Boy? Shame the TV broke before he got a chance to show us what other colors he can turn."

This time Mary didn't laugh.

"The TV didn't break; he made that happen. Timothy's got tele-tech: he can control electrical stuff. Or he will be able to when he's trained properly."

Murph's brain was working overtime. "And I suppose Nellie can change the color of her hair and shut windows on demand?"

"No!" Mary actually stamped her foot. "That would be silly."

"Thank goodness, because this whole thing was really starting to get freaky."

"She can control storm clouds."

"Right. Obviously. So, what's the next lesson? Climbing buildings and shooting webs out of my wrist?"

"No, actually it's double math."

"Moon math or normal-person math?"

"Just math, Murph," sniffed Mary, before turning away from him and disappearing into the girls' bathroom. "This is still a school, you know. Not much good being able to fly if you can't add, is it?"

Fly . . . ? Murph thought back to his mom's conversation with Mr. Souperman the previous week. Everything was becoming clear, but not in a good way. It was like unfogging the car windshield only to discover you were about to drive off a cliff. *Holy guacamole*, he thought to himself, suddenly not looking forward to tomorrow's Capability Training lesson one little bit . . .

These people think I can actually fly.

* * *

For years now, Murph and his mom had had an agreement. No, more than an agreement: a *pact*. She wasn't allowed to ask the question. You know the one: the mom question. The one to which there is only one possible answer.

The question is this: "Soooo," (and the mom can drag this word out for several seconds) "how was school?"

The time-honored answer is, "Um, okay, I suppose," but it must be delivered within 0.25 seconds, so it usually sounds more like "murkyspose." Murph had made his mom agree, on threat of sulks, not to ask the question any more.

So, that evening, after picking a silent Murph up from The School, driving him home in silence, and eating silent sausage, wordless mashed potatoes, and taciturn beans, Murph's mom simply sat there with her eyebrows raised and waited for Murph to give her the verdict.

Andy was sleeping over at a friend's house, which should have made things a bit easier, but each line Murph rehearsed in his head seemed worse than the last. Where on earth should he start?

So, you know this new school? Well, turns out it's a

*special, secret school for kids with superpowers. Weird,
eh? Anyway, I haven't got any powers so the first lesson
tomorrow's going to be a bit of a challenge . . .*

So, I made friends with someone who can fly . . .

*Mom, I really need to ask you about girls. Is it normal
for them to conjure thunderstorms out of thin air . . . ?*

So, instead, Murph stayed silent. And his mom gazed
at him with an encouraging expression on her face that
looked as if it might crumble into pieces at any moment.
Only it didn't.

Murph looked back at his mom and managed to
force a small smile. He was remembering the advice
she always gave him when things felt unmanageable.
Problems don't go away on their own, she would tell him.
*But problems are cowards and bullies, and they only take
advantage if they think they can win. Face them. Look them
in the eye. Show them you're not scared. If you show them
you're not scared of them, they'll run away.*

And so, with those words in mind, at school the next
morning Murph summoned every ounce of courage he
had in his body, including the small amount usually

stored in his toes, and said the words before he could give himself a chance to back out.

"I am not, in fact," he declared in a loud, confident voice, **"able to fly."**

It was the beginning of the daily Capability Training lesson, and Murph had decided to face his problems head-on. Mr. Flash had called him to the front of the class, and before the instructor had time to clear the chairs away, Murph had stopped him with a raised hand and told the whole class that he had something to share.

It wasn't going over well.

"What on earth are you doing at this school, then?" sputtered Mr. Flash, his head going so red it looked like a tomato with a mustache stuck on the front. Murph took a deep breath. It was time to come clean.

"I have literally no idea," he said in a quiet but firm voice. "I have made friends with a girl who, apparently, can fly. She is sitting next to another girl who can control storm clouds. Timothy here"—he gestured at Timothy, who was looking at him as if he were a small and not especially attractive caterpillar—"can make electronics fry, and she . . . she . . . ," Murph continued, pointing at

44

a curly-haired young lady in the second row. "Actually, I have no idea what she can do."

"I'm Hilda, and I can summon two tiny horses," she said nervously.

"Right, Hilda here is a . . . is a horse, um, a tiny horse summoner. I, on the other hand, am just a normal kid."

Mr. Flash really did look as if he was about to pop. He appeared to be speechless, which made him, if anything, even more like an actual tomato. Suddenly he seemed almost to vanish as he activated his own Capability—incredible speed. He flashed to the back of the classroom and peered at Murph from a distance. Then papers blew from desks as he raced back to the front so that they were practically standing nose to nose.

"A NORMAL KID?" he bellowed at the top of his voice.

The class erupted into shrieks of delighted laughter. One or two of Timothy's friends started chanting, and it quickly caught on: **"Normal kid! Normal kid! Normal kid!"**

"SILENCE!" roared Mr. Flash, zipping around the class like a red-tipped tornado, trying to restore order. But he'd lost control, and he wasn't the only one.

As he'd explained to his students on day one, it takes concentration to keep your Capability in check. And concentration had gone right out the window. With a tinkling, neighing sound, two tiny white horses materialized out of thin air and galloped across the desktops. The replacement TV, which was standing in the corner, exploded, and a huge clap of thunder sounded outside. A tallish boy in a blue top on the other side of the classroom emitted a small noise like a balloon being let go, and his head inflated to four times its normal size.

Amid the chaos, the chanting continued. But gradually the words seemed to get jumbled up, and before long it sounded as if the class was chanting something else. The name, in fact, that Murph Cooper was to be known by from that day onward . . .

"Kid normal, kid normal, KID NORMAL!"

Twenty minutes later, Mr. Souperman was looking stressed. He'd just been given some very disturbing news. "No powers . . . at all?" he wondered, furrowing his brow.

"No, sir, none whatsoever," replied Mr. Flash. The CT teacher was standing in front of Mr. Souperman's desk with his legs apart and his hands behind his back. "I thought he was joking at first, but it's true. Kid Normal, they've started calling him. Teasing him."

The headmaster thought back to his conversation with Murph's mom in the street outside The School at the end of the previous week and realized that he'd made a rather stupid error—but he hadn't come to be in charge of a top-secret school by owning up to his mistakes.

"Well . . ." He gazed out the window, pretending to ponder. "There's obviously been a screw-up somewhere along the line, hasn't there?"

The headmaster turned back to face Mr. Flash, thinking fast and considering his options. What would happen if he admitted he'd enrolled a non-super child in his school by accident? He'd be fired before he could say, "Whoops, I stupidly admitted a non-super kid to my super school because of a misunderstanding over the word 'fly.'"

On the other hand, what would happen if Murph was allowed to stay? What would it be like for The School? What would it be like for Murph?

Like most leaders throughout history at one point or another, Mr. Souperman was hoping desperately that someone else would solve the problem for him.

"What do *you* think I should do, Mr. Flash?" he mused fake-casually.

To Mr. Flash, the answer was as plain as the bushy mustache on his face.

"Kick 'im out!" he said meanly. "We've never had a kid with no Capability at this school. It would be a travesty. A kid without a Cape is like a swan . . ." He paused, trying to work out what the most important part of a swan was.

"Yes, Mr. Flash . . . ?" said Mr. Souperman.

"Like a swan," Mr. Flash concluded decisively, unable to think of anything a swan had. "A swan. Never had a swan in The School either. You'd kick *it* out, wouldn't you?"

Mr. Souperman rolled his eyes and turned to look out the window again, unable to shake the image of Mr. Flash booting a swan out of The School gates. Strangely entertaining though it was, this pleasing mental picture was not helping him make a decision, so he turned back around and adopted his most dramatic face as Mr. Flash continued to plead with him: "No one without a Cape has ever been allowed to have anything to do with this school."

The headmaster stopped him there. "Well, there has been one, of course," he said.

"Oh, *him*? He doesn't count," spat Mr. Flash.

Mr. Souperman needed time to think. "Well, thanks for your input, Mr. Flash. I'll decide what to do in due time." And with that he sat down, wondering desperately how he could kick Murph out of The School now, without it becoming obvious that he'd made a gigantic error by allowing him to come there in the first place.

Mr. Flash made a cross **hrummph** noise, looking for all the world as though he was about to go and find a swan to kick. Then, abruptly, he seemed to blur and vanish as his Cape activated once again. Moving so fast that the human eye was unable to track him, he left the room like a blast of angry wind and was **hrummph**-ing in his own classroom at the other end of the building within seconds. Mr. Souperman, who had superhuman strength but perhaps only average human intelligence, didn't even notice that Mr. Flash had stolen a cookie on his way out.

6

Nektar's Genesis

SIX MONTHS EARLIER ...
If you are reading this story out loud, at this point please make a noise with your mouth that indicates we are traveling back in time six months.

Louder.

Louder ...

Now do a sort of swooshy noise. Now quack like a duck. Now make a noise like a seal being run over by a combine harvester.

Ha ha, we can make you do anything!

Clive Meeke, the most brilliant young researcher at Ribbon Robotics, sat in his laboratory with his head in his hands. Outside, night was falling, and the yellowish glow of a streetlight shining through the blinds cast striped shadows across the back of his lab coat. The room was silent except for a blatting, buzzing noise that came from a large glass jar surrounded by wires and electrical circuits attached to it with black rubber pads.

Without warning, the door burst open.

"Well, Meeke?" purred the tall woman silhouetted in the doorway. "You promised me results by six o'clock. It's now quarter to seven."

With time-telling like that, you could really see how this woman had risen to the very top of her profession. For this was Arabella Ribbon, head of the entire company. She flicked back her hair, stunning a passing fly.

"I'm terribly sorry, Miss Ribbon," stammered the young man, struggling to his feet. "I calculated all the variables time and time again, but the sequencer just won't read them."

"You promised me that you could use the DNA of insects to create a new, more efficient kind of robot brain," hissed Arabella, conveniently summing up what was going on. "And I've paid you very well for more than a year now. I want results! I don't care if you have to stay here all night. If I don't see some progress when I come into this office at nine o'clock tomorrow morning, you're fired!"

"Yes, yes, of course, Miss Ribbon, thank you," said Meeke, cringing. The door slammed and he slumped back into his chair.

After a few minutes he turned and tapped a few keys on an old-fashioned computer. Green numbers scrolled upward on the screen, and Meeke narrowed his eyes. He rolled his chair over to the glass jar and peered inside. A single wasp was climbing up the side, fluttering its wings weakly.

"Why can't I read you?" muttered Meeke. "What are you hiding from me? What goes on inside that insect brain?"

Suddenly a thought struck him, and he stood up abruptly. "If the sequencer can't read your wasp mind, I wonder . . . can it read any brain waves at all?" he murmured. He detached two of the pads from the outside of the glass jar and clamped them to his own temples. The wasp buzzed angrily at the disturbance.

Meeke flicked a switch on the wall, and a low hum started up. He turned back to the computer and typed in a few numbers.

The screen went blank, and then a single word appeared:

SEQUENCING . . .

But for a long time, nothing else happened.

"Let's increase the power, shall we?" mused Meeke, tapping in a few more numbers, then, after another minute, a few more. The humming increased in volume, and the buzzing of the wasp grew more frantic.

"Still nothing," snapped the scientist, adjusting the

rubber pads on his head and tapping more buttons. "Maximum power!"

The hum became a scream, which mingled with the frenzied drumming of the wasp's wings. The electrical circuits attached to the glass jar glowed orange, and Clive Meeke shrieked in pain. There was a sharp crack, a bright flash, and all the lights in the building went out.

Now there was no sound. The glow of the streetlight fell on an empty desk, illuminating nothing but a

slowly spinning plume of smoke as it rose from the burned husk of a wasp in the shattered remains of the glass jar.

Arabella Ribbon once again displayed her excellent clock-reading skills by bossing her way through the door of Meeke's laboratory at exactly nine o'clock the following morning. She was greeted by three things.

First, the lingering scent of burned wasp, which is one of the worst smells, right up there with egg sandwiches and pee on a hot barbecue. Second, the sight of millions of dollars worth of electronic and computing equipment that had been broken and smashed into pieces, then mashed together into what could only be described as a nest. It filled the space between the workbench and the window, which still had the blinds drawn across it.

And in the middle of that nest was sitting the third thing to greet her. It was wearing the tattered remains of Clive Meeke's white lab coat.

But this couldn't possibly be the young robotics engineer she'd been looking forward to having a really good shout at. Meeke had been cowardly and craven. This person was sitting with his back to her, calmly humming—or more like *buzzing*—an eerie little tune.

"Meeke?" she said nervously.

"Don't look so nervous," drawled the thing in the nest. "I promised you results, and I think this is really going to blow . . . your . . . mind."

"What do you mean, 'look nervous'?" said Arabella, straightening her back and remembering just who was the boss around there. "You can't even see me."

"Oh, but I *can* see you, Bella. In fact my vision has improved ALL AROUND."

The man spun sharply in his chair, knocking over a conical flask and smashing it to pieces, which added to the drama. As he slowly rose to his feet, Arabella gasped. Whereas Clive Meeke had two weedy-looking brown eyes, this . . . *creature* had two enormous bulging insect eyes. She could see her increasingly pale face reflected in them many times over.

"What are you doing, Meeke?" she shrieked as he advanced on her.

"Meeke? Meeke? Clive Meeke is no more! He's . . .
flown the hive, you might say."

"Isn't it bees that live in a hive? You look more like
a wasp," said Arabella.

"Silence!" roared the wasp. "You may have been
queen around here, but it's time this swarm had a new
leader."

"Again, I think that's bees . . . ," began Arabella, but

it was too late. The creature reached out toward her and she saw with horror a sharp, glittering stinger protruding from the inside of each wrist.

He lunged at her before she had time to think about escaping, the stings thrusting out farther with venom dripping from the tips. Luckily for us, Arabella Ribbon's scream of pure terror was cut short abruptly as the paragraph ended.

We now ask you to fast-forward six months. If you're reading this story out loud, we would like you to indicate this by making a fast-forwarding sound. To perform this accurately, you must do the following: open the nearest window and shout at the top of your voice, "I AM THE PRINCE OF THE POODLE PARLOR!"

There we go. It doesn't sound anything like a fast-forward, but didn't it feel great?

Anyway, Your Majesty, in many ways, we're back to where we were a few pages ago, but this time, crucially, we know how the evil Nektar came to be. And you are now in charge of all poodles. Congratulations. You may read on.

7

A School for Heroes

As the day wore on, it became clear to Murph that the story of his dramatic announcement in the CT lesson had spread through The School like wildfire; people were passing it on faster than head lice. And yet, despite this newfound fame, Murph felt very alone. This should have been a pretty normal feeling for him. At his last school he'd spent a lot of time on his own, and after a while the other kids had more or less left him to it. But being alone at The School was an entirely new experience, because here, nobody would stop staring at him.

Even in a school full of weirdos who can inflate their own heads, I'M the outcast, he thought to himself glumly.

He didn't even feel like he could call on his new pal Mary, because, for all he knew, she might want to distance herself too, now that he'd revealed he wasn't a skimmer like her. A couple of times he'd seen her walking his way with a determined expression, but he was so embarrassed that he'd kept his head down and managed to avoid her.

Murph's presence at The School seemed to be a constant topic of conversation, and during the day—whether between classes, at break time, lunchtime, any time really—there was constant side-eyeing and whispering. He pretended it wasn't about him and tried to ignore it, but that was easier said than done. Particularly when some people decided to confront him directly during an otherwise uneventful math class.

"How did you even end up here, Kid Normal?" asked TV exploder Timothy aggressively.

Murph shook his head, wishing he had a decent answer. He couldn't face embarrassing himself even more by telling the lame truth again. After math, the class shuffled along to their next period, everybody avoiding Murph as if he had three heads, all of which had chicken pox.

But before they could reach the next classroom, the ax that had been hovering over Murph's head for the last hour fell. "Who's Cooper?" a voice shouted.

Murph looked up. Two much older students were coming down the hallway toward him.

Now what? he thought.

They were impressive-looking creatures, a boy and a girl. The boy was handsome, dressed in a cool jacket; the girl was wearing sunglasses and had long, straight black hair. Murph noticed she was fiddling with some sort of phone with a green light on it, but she put it away as she approached the class.

"Cooper?" she repeated. "Which one's Cooper?"

There was no need for him to answer. Everyone else had retreated, leaving him on his own in the middle of the hallway like a sad island.

"Come on," said the wavy-haired boy, "headmaster's office." He gestured over his shoulder with a thumb and marched off.

The others, who were watching from a distance, started mumbling as Murph was ushered away. "Do you think he's in for it?" someone whispered. "Back to normal school for Kid Normal," said another voice as he turned the corner. "What's going to happen to him?" someone else asked. The whole class was quietly simmering with nosey excitement and speculation as he trudged off.

This is it, thought Murph as he shuffled down the corridor. At least he could claim the world record for Shortest Stay Ever at a Weird School for Weirdos. He suddenly felt frustrated he would never get to know more: he was bewildered by it all, sure, but this school was the most interesting place he'd been in ages. And much like you'd do before leaving for the airport at the end of a vacation, he took one last fond look at his surroundings before they were just a surreal memory.

They headed past classrooms where the next classes were just beginning. He could hear teachers' voices, and as he passed one room there was a loud bang and a gasp from his soon-to-be-ex-classmates. The old janitor hurried down the hallway with a fire extinguisher and looked at Murph quizzically. Murph noticed the name "Carl" written on the white embroidered patch on his blue overalls.

"Just in case," Carl shouted over his shoulder, barging through the classroom door with the extinguisher at the ready.

After a while, Murph's two companions stopped to give him his final directions. "Straight down the main hall to the end and up the stairs. It's the round part that looks out over the soccer fields. You know it?"

Murph had indeed noticed a turret-like structure tacked onto the edge of what were otherwise pretty conventional-looking school buildings, and he began climbing cheerlessly to the top of it.

Slightly out of breath, Murph arrived outside Mr. Souperman's study. He found himself in a small, cluttered waiting area lined with bookcases. The tops of these bookcases held a selection of rather strange ornaments. There were a few carved wooden animals, but Murph also noticed what looked like a shark's jawbone and a black metal dial that could have come from an old-fashioned airplane. A yellowing poster showing a snowy mountaintop was tacked to the wall, beside a black-and-white photograph of a large waterfall.

It was as though he'd wandered into a junk shop by mistake, but he didn't say that to the old lady who was sitting at a desk in the middle of all the clutter. It would have been rude. Instead he gave the international noise for "Please stop tapping at your laptop and look at me"—which sounds exactly like a small, nervous cough.

The lady stopped tapping at her laptop and looked up at him. She had fluffy white hair that made her head look like someone had smeared it with glue and rolled it in cotton wool. (But you shouldn't do that to old ladies; it's cruel.) Her eyes, set inside deltas of wrinkles, were very bright and seemed kind.

"Hi," she said to Murph simply.

"Hello," replied Murph, "I'm here to see . . . you know . . ."

"Mr. Souperman? He won't be a minute. It's Murph, isn't it?" He nodded. "Have a seat for a bit, why don't you?" Murph looked around and saw a row of hard plastic stools in front of one of the bookcases. Once he was uncomfortably seated, an uncomfortable silence grew, just to add to the general air of uncomfort.

The lady with white hair, whose name was Flora, by the way, although she hasn't told us that yet, didn't go back to her typing—instead she gazed at Murph intently

as he balanced on his plastic perch like the world's unluckiest gnome.

"Well, you're one for the books, aren't you?" she said after a moment.

Murph only raised his eyebrows in reply.

"How did you manage to end up here, I wonder?" she went on absently, almost to herself.

She smiled at him, and her kind face crinkled up like a friendly, crumpled bag of chips—and suddenly Murph was telling her everything. His mom's job, the friends he missed, the awful new house: it all came spilling out. As he spoke, he realized that he'd wanted to say a lot of this out loud to his mom for a long time. But he'd been keeping it bottled up, as he knew she felt guilty enough as it was. But now he just couldn't help himself. This nice, grandma-ish lady had appeared, and he let it rip.

"And now that they've found out I don't have one of these dumb 'Capabilities,' I suppose they're going to throw me out," he finished.

For a nightmarish moment, Murph thought he might be about to cry, but he'd become an expert at cutting that feeling off and pulled himself together just in time. The white-haired lady smiled at him again.

"Well, you're quite the worrier, aren't you? But it always helps to have a chat about it, I find." She inclined her head respectfully. "Picking the right people to share your worries with—that's the important bit. These things have a way of coming out in the wash anyway," she went on, which is the sort of thing that older ladies often say.

In fact, it was a favorite saying of Murph's grandma, though he hardly ever got to hear her say it because they'd had to move so far away.

"My name's Flora, by the way," confirmed Flora. "You'll usually find me here outside the headmaster's office—so if you feel it's all getting on top of you, you come and let me know, all right? I'm here to listen if you need me. I'll go and see if he's ready." Flora gave him a reassuring wink and disappeared through the headmaster's office door.

Even though he was still convinced he was about to be told to find a new school, Murph had started to feel about 2 percent better, which was a significant improvement on the last few weeks and took him to a grand total of 5 percent. But it *had* been good to talk to someone about it all, he realized.

He sighed and prepared himself as Flora came back out of the office and gestured to him encouragingly. When he stepped inside, Flora nodded kindly, shuffled out and closed the door behind her.

"Ah yes, Mr. Cooper, come in, come in," said the headmaster, ushering Murph over to his desk and striding across to a window, which he'd decided to stare out of in order to appear more impressive. Murph just thought he was being odd, and as he didn't have a face to look at, his gaze wandered around the room, taking in his surroundings.

The office was round, with large picture windows on all sides overlooking the fields at the back of The School and the patch of woods behind them. In between the windows was a series of framed pictures of a much younger Mr. Souperman in a tight-fitting red costume. One showed him shaking hands with a lady with puffy hair in a neat blue suit outside a black door with a number ten on it. In another, he was holding a small kitten and looking very pleased with himself. A third showed him with his hands on his hips, one foot planted on what appeared to be a gigantic unconscious clown. A collapsed and scorched circus tent smoldered in the background.

Mr. Souperman spun around and saw Murph staring. "Party Animal, he called himself. Catchphrase: 'It's my party and you'll die if I want you to.' Nasty piece of work. Do have a seat."

Murph sank into one of three comfortable leather chairs that were arranged in front of the large wooden desk. The desk was bare except for a phone that looked very much like the one the girl with sunglasses had been using—but it wasn't a model Murph recognized. Mr. Souperman turned away from him again and gazed out over the grounds.

"I expect this all seems a little strange to you, Mr. Cooper."

Murph nodded, thinking privately that the word "strange" didn't even begin to cover it.

"You and your, ah, charming mother have stumbled across a school that is not for ordinary children."

This is it, thought Murph. *This is where they call Mom and get her to pick me up, and we start Operation School Search all over again.*

"But, after much deliberation, I have decided that I will allow you to stay with us for the time being. After all, a touch of outside perspective might help our little community," blustered Mr. Souperman. Murph had no idea what was going on—but he kept his mouth shut, which was a tactic that had often served him well.

At this point Mr. Souperman turned back around once more to face him. His arms seemed to be bulging more than usual underneath his gray jacket. It looked as if his biceps might make a bid for freedom at any moment.

"I just need to know," he said, fixing Murph with a steely gaze, "that we can count on your discretion."

Based on the earlier "flying" episode, which got him into this sticky pudding of a problem to begin with, Murph thought it would be best to ask for clarity: "When you say 'discretion,' what exactly are we talking about?"

Mr. Souperman picked up a cup of coffee that had been sitting on the windowsill and drained it. It had gone cold and tasted disgusting, but he hid it well.

"I mean . . . ," Murph continued, "do you mean that if I accidentally let slip a couple of things about what goes on at this school to my mom, you'll be slightly miffed?"

"Not quite, Mr. Cooper," replied Mr. Souperman with a raise of an eyebrow and a ripple of an arm.

"Or is it more like 'Don't, under any circumstances, breathe a word to anyone about the secret school or you'll be killed'?" suggested Murph.

"HA HA!" replied Mr. Souperman, banging a hand on his desk and denting it. The smile suddenly vanished from his face. "Yes, the latter." He seemed to relent slightly. "Well, probably not killed," he added kindly, "but certainly, um . . . well, as I say, I'm sure we can count on your discretion."

There was a silence as if they'd both forgotten their lines in a terrible school play. Murph volunteered the start of one. "I—"

He was cut off immediately. It wasn't his turn to speak.

"Cooper. It's perfectly simple. Do not tell anyone outside of The School about The School. Do you understand?"

There was a crunching noise as Mr. Souperman absentmindedly crushed his coffee cup into a fine powder with one hand, before pouring the remains into the trash. Murph thought he got the message.

8

The Ultra Spoon

Ribbon Robotics headquarters was situated on the outskirts of the town, at the edge of a large and mostly deserted industrial park. The company's founder had chosen it deliberately because it was so isolated; Arabella Ribbon had been developing a range of combat drones, which she was hoping to sell to the army.

Her grand idea was that her flying robots could be sent out onto the battlefield to fight instead of soldiers, communicating with one another like electronic insects. But of course Arabella Ribbon wasn't in charge any more. And in the six months since she had disappeared, company policy had changed.

On the top floor of the Ribbon Robotics headquarters was a long, bright room that Arabella had used to hold meetings. But in the large leather chair she used to occupy at one end of the room, there now sat a repulsive-looking creature. Once he had been a young robotics engineer called Clive Meeke. But he was using a different name these days.

"All hail Nektar!" proclaimed his servant, whose name was Gary, entering the room carrying a tray loaded with sweet fizzy drinks.

In fact, Gary wasn't really a servant; he was a student who'd been sent to Ribbon Robotics on an internship placement. He was supposed to be spending three months learning how a real working robotics factory operated. Instead, on his first day, he'd been ushered into Nektar's presence, which had been quite a shock. But when a man who appears to be half wasp announces that you are now his personal servant, it's probably just as well to agree.

Bright sunshine streamed through the windows that lined the length of the boardroom. Nektar's bulbous black eyes seemed to greedily suck in the sight of the brightly colored cans of drink, and he reached out a long-fingered hand and selected one. He opened it and held it up at chest height.

Gary tried not to look too repulsed as a long, flexible

tongue flopped out of Nektar's mouth and began to slurp at the sickly sweet liquid. It was truly gross.

"All-powerful Nektar," began Gary, swallowing back a small globule of vomit that had forced its way up to the back of his throat, "the applicants are waiting in the antechamber whenever you are ready to receive them."

For Nektar, taking over the robotics factory had just been the start. He was simply buzzing with evil schemes, and now he'd decided to appoint a second-in-command to help implement them.

Of course, most of the staff at the factory weren't aware they were now working for the product of a hideously botched experiment that had fused the brain waves and DNA of a man with those of a wasp. They'd probably have complained to Human Resources about it. No, they thought they still worked for the haughty and unavailable Arabella Ribbon, who'd never been much of a mingler at the best of times and now seemed to be more reclusive than ever. But a few carefully chosen members of staff knew the truth, and it was from these select few that he was going to pick his head henchperson.

Apart from anything else, Nektar had thought, making them go through a stressful interview would completely take up the middle of their day. And if there's one thing that wasps love, it's spoiling people's lunch.

"Should I send them through to the boardroom?" asked Gary.

"Not yet!" snapped Nektar in his petulant, reedy, buzzing voice. "Go through to the antechamber and I shall summon them when I am ready."

By now his long, hollow tongue was getting to the end of the first can of soda, and it made that horrible plughole noise as it slurped up the last drops. Gary's cheeks bulged. He bowed and left the room.

Nektar waited for a few seconds, then leaned forward to the intercom on the desk in front of him. He pressed the button.

"Are you in the antechamber yet, Gary?" There was silence.

Nektar snapped open another can of soda. He tried to wait patiently and lasted about three seconds.

"*Gary!*" he shouted, jabbing the intercom button again.

"Yes, all-powerful Nektar?" said the intern kid. His voice was distorted by the speaker, but he still sounded like he'd just been sick in a potted plant.

"Send the candidates through to the boardroom, would you?" buzzed Nektar. He leaned back in his chair like a great, sugar-crazed loon. *This ought to be fun*, he thought.

After a moment, three people trooped through the double doors and stood at the other end of the room. Each placed an object covered with a white cloth on the table in front of them.

Two of the candidates—a woman and a man—were

dressed in white lab coats. The third, a pale man with a pointed nose and carefully arranged hair, was wearing a slick suit and very shiny black shoes that ended in sharp points. They were the sort of shoes you should never trust. He brushed some dust off his chair before sitting down carefully, pulling at the front of his pants so as not to spoil their creases. The other two looked nervous, fiddling with the files they'd brought in with them, but he gazed coolly at Nektar and waited politely for him to begin speaking.

"Welcome, my trusted servants," began Nektar. "As you know, I have decided to honor one of you with a very special opportunity." He broke off and sucked ravenously at his can of soda. "But this job can only go to one who is worthy. Who among you can impress me enough to become my head henchman? Person! Hench*person*!" he corrected himself quickly, seeing the female candidate bristling. Even a giant wasp needs to know where to draw the line. "Who wants to go first?"

The white-coated man took the opportunity and stood up. He was a twitchy kind of person, with food stains down his front, thick black-rimmed glasses, and hair that looked like it had gone crazy. Oh, and he had a strong German accent, which was odd as he'd actually grown up about a mile away and had never been to Germany to his life. We've just put it in to keep you on your toes.

"My name," he began (in his strong German accent, remember—no slacking), "is Professor Graham Smith. And I would like to share with you my dastardly evil invention. **Behold!**"

At this, he whipped the cloth in front of him away, revealing a decidedly normal-looking spoon with a red button on the handle.

"The Ultra Spoon!" gloated Smith, looking around

in triumph at the other two candidates. "Never again will we suffer the indignity of stirring our own coffee." He tried to think of another word for "behold" but couldn't, and instead shouted, "Because!" for no reason.

The room fell silent. Someone coughed.

With a dramatic flourish, Smith pressed the button on the spoon, and there was a tiny whizzing noise as the end of it began to spin around. Smith laughed delightedly, only stopping when Nektar got to his feet, leaped around the table, and stung him unconscious. It was only

a little sting, mind you. But Smith suddenly took on the demeanor of a businessman who had fallen asleep on the last train home after one too many drinks at the Christmas party. He slumped sideways off his chair, dribbling.

"**Next!**" Nektar yelled at the top of his voice.

"Penny Percival, evil Lord Nektar," said the female candidate primly. "As you know, I have been in charge of your robotic insect program. Using your research, we have developed a fleet of spy drones to do your bidding. To the human eye they are almost indistinguishable from normal wasps. But, in fact, each contains a sophisticated camera, microphone, and guidance system. They are the most advanced spy robots ever built."

She glanced smugly at the motionless form of Graham Smith on the floor beside her, where he was collecting a sizable puddle of drool around his mouth. Nektar smiled.

"But what I have to show you today is something else altogether," she continued. "I have become a little concerned that we haven't really been doing much to help the planet . . ."

The smile instantly vanished from Nektar's face. Unfazed by this, Penny removed the white cloth in front of her to reveal a bowl with a single rainbow-striped fish in the bottom of it. Beside it was a glass jar of foul-looking brownish sludge.

"This robot fish is the answer to all the world's clean water problems," announced Penny. "Please observe."

She tipped the stinking liquid into the fish bowl, and through the murk, Nektar's bulbous eyes could just make out the small fish beginning to swim backward and forward. The pointy-shoed man leaned forward with interest.

Gradually, as the fish swam around, the liquid in the bowl began to clear, until a few minutes later the fish was swimming contentedly in perfectly clean water, an adorable smile on its face. To anyone who wasn't an evil wasp-based hybrid, this would be the most remarkable thing in the whole world.

But, sadly, Nektar *was* evil, and so he hated it. He jumped up, darted to the other end of the table, grabbed the fish out of its bowl, and stamped on it repeatedly, yelling, "What"—**STAMP**—"is the point"—**STAMP**—"of that? How am I supposed to be a supervillain"—**STAMP**—"if all I do is clean people's ponds?" **STAMPSTAMPSTAMP.**

Penny Percival gathered up the remains of her miraculous fish and ran from the room in tears.

Nektar returned to his seat, laced his hands behind his head, and turned his attention wordlessly to the sharply dressed man.

"Knox, sir. Nicholas Knox," the man said. "I joined the company three months ago to work on your personal robot strike force and have been eager to meet with you. Your reputation precedes you."

For a man who'd just watched one of his colleagues get stung until he passed out and another have her invention stamped on repeatedly, Knox didn't seem nervous. He had indeed only started at Ribbon Robotics recently, but had risen quickly up the ranks with a delicate combination of oiliness and acidity, like a sneaky salad dressing. He flicked a lock of his carefully arranged hair back from his face, and calmly removed the white cloth from his own invention.

It looked not unlike a yellow-and-black-striped bicycle

helmet, though it was thinner and more delicate. But this was no ordinary bicycle helmet, as Knox was about to reveal.

"This is no ordinary bicycle helmet," he confirmed. "I wonder if we might have a volunteer, sir?"

Nektar pressed his intercom. "Gary, would you step in here a moment?"

There was silence.

Impatiently, Nektar strode to the door and flung it open. "Gary!" he bellowed at the top of his voice.

"Yes, my lord?" replied Gary, who was squatting on a small stool in the corridor in case he was needed.

"Go to the intercom in the antechamber," commanded Nektar.

"But I'm already here, your waspishness," began Gary desperately, before seeing the expression on Nektar's face and scuttling away.

Nektar returned to his chair. He waited a moment, then pressed the button in front of him again: "Gary, would you step in here a moment?"

"Yes, Lord Nektar," replied Gary, secretly rolling his eyes. A moment later, he traipsed back into the boardroom. "How can I be of service, sir?"

"Try this on for size," Knox instructed. Gary did as he was told and carefully placed the black-and-yellow hat onto his head.

"It fits!" he exclaimed.

"Of course it fits," replied a smug-looking Knox. "It's a one-size-fits-all mind-control helmet . . ."

"A what-control helmet?" squeaked Gary.

"Nothing!" fluted Knox guiltily. "Now, Mr. Gary," he went on. "Your challenge is a simple one. I'd like you to run at the wall as fast as you possibly can."

"What? I'm not doing that. It'll hurt," said Gary.

Knox reached up and pushed a button on the back of the helmet. Lights flickered into life along both sides of it, and immediately Gary's eyes widened and, more worryingly, changed color. The whites had become a bright yellow, with huge black pupils in the center.

"Now, let's try again, shall we?" said Knox forcefully. "Drone, I want you to run at the wall as fast as you can," he repeated.

Immediately Gary ran at full speed straight into the wall. His face hit it with a *crack* and he fell to the floor, unconscious.

Nektar roared with delighted laughter: "He's been Knoxed out cold!"

"Ah! Good one, sir," lied Knox. "So, as you can see, I've managed to find a way of controlling the human brain. I can make anyone do anything."

"You mean . . . WE can make anyone do anything?" said Nektar.

"Yes, that's what I said, sir," said Knox, with a twitch at the corner of his mouth. "We can make anyone do anything. So, do I get the job?"

"Oh yes," said Nektar greedily as he reached out for the helmet that Knox had removed from the motionless Gary. "Welcome to the hive, Knox."

"That's bees, you idiot," sighed Knox, but not loudly enough for Nektar to hear.

9

The Alliance

It's always a strange experience walking into class late. It's even stranger when you've just gone to see the headmaster and he's threatened you with physical violence.

Murph headed back to the room where he'd left the rest of his class and creaked open the door, which seemed like the loudest noise on earth. Every single head in the room turned toward him as he scuttled in sideways like an unusually shy crab. He noticed several different expressions as he went to his seat: surprise, confusion, annoyance, and really needing to pee. This last one had nothing to do with him. Murph couldn't have known this, but Sophie Clark's parents insisted she drink two gallons of water every day.

"Welcome, welcome," said the teacher at the front of the class, who was sitting at a large grand piano. As she said each word, she played a chord, which gave Murph the impression he had walked into *Weirdo School: The Musical.*

The tinkling teacher was The School's head of music, Mrs. Baum.

"Today I'm going to be playing you one of my favorite pieces of music," continued Mrs. Baum. "As I was just saying, Elgar's 'Nimrod' is all about friendship, and how your friends can inspire you."

This was literally music to Murph's ears. It almost sounded like a normal lesson, and after being allowed to stay at The School by the skin of his teeth, any class where he might be able to make head or tail of what was going on was a bonus. He sank gratefully behind an empty desk.

"Now, have a listen as I play the piece for you," said Mrs. Baum in soothing tones. She cracked her knuckles and lifted her hands above the keys. Nearby, Murph noticed Mary wince.

Mrs. Baum froze for a moment, as if gathering her thoughts, then began to play. And immediately Murph realized that, of course, this was nothing like a normal lesson. Here at The School, the teachers had Capes just like their students. Mrs. Baum's was the ability to move her hands with lightning speed. She finished Elgar's lovely, inspiring piece of music in just under two seconds.

It sounded like . . . well, it's difficult to describe what it sounded like. It sounded like someone was pressing five thousand notes at once. It sounded like a musical nosebleed. It sounded like a really fat otter had scurried across the piano keys on its way to an otter party.

Mrs. Baum opened her eyes and looked expectantly at her class. "What did you think?" she asked them innocently.

Murph looked around blankly, then bowed his head until it touched the desk in front of him. He sighed a sigh that actually lasted longer than Mrs. Baum's Elgar concert.

The lesson ended twenty minutes later, after Mrs. Baum had played them the complete high-speed works of Mozart, Beethoven, Strauss, and, oddly, several TV theme tunes from the 1980s. Everyone spilled out into the hallway, wondering how they were ever going to learn anything about music . . . and what on earth was *Press Your Luck*?

Murph heard several mutterings. "What you still doing here, Kid Normal?" asked Timothy as he and his friends jostled past him. The rest of the class seemed to have decided to ignore him, and the hallway quickly emptied. Only Mary stayed behind, along with Hilda the tiny horse girl, though she didn't seem eager to hang around either. "Hang on," he heard Mary hiss to her as they approached him.

"Right, what on earth is going on?" Mary asked Murph, giving him the full raised-eyebrow treatment. "Why did you tell me you could fly?"

"Actually, I didn't ever tell anyone I can fly," replied Murph matter-of-factly. "I think you asked me if I was a skimmer, and I had no idea what you were talking about."

Mary pursed her lips and looked at him with her head on one side. "You are a puzzle, aren't you? So what happened with Mr. Souperman? We thought when Deborah Lamington came and dragged you off to his office, you were going to be kicked out."

"Deborah what-ington?"

Hilda piped up. "Deborah Lamington—she's, like, the coolest girl in The School. Her and Dirk—that's the boy who was with her—are actually *operational*. Someone was telling me about it in the bathroom the other day. They're, like, so awesome."

"All right, Hilda, calm down," said Mary. "They're not that cool. Hilda wants to be a Hero, you see," she continued to Murph. "She's desperate to get noticed by the Alliance—"

"Whatareyoutalkingabout?" blurted Murph, cutting into the stream of gibberish. "Okay—can we start from the beginning, please? I have quite literally no idea what is going on. I have ended up at this school by accident. So humor me, okay? Start with the basics, and every time you say something I don't understand, I'm going to hoot like a confused owl."

Mary looked at him with exasperation, then seemed to relent and smiled. "Fine, we'll start from the beginning. I told you about Capes, right?"

"Right," confirmed Murph.

"Short for 'Capabilities,'" Hilda added excitedly.

"Hoooot?" said Owl Murph.

"If you find out you have a Capability, you're invited to come to a school like this one, where they train you to use it—and more importantly to hide it," Mary said.

"T-wooot?" asked the owl. "How does The School know you have a superpower?"

"'CAPE'!" Hilda corrected him.

"Well, it's secret, of course," said Mary, "but I think they have contacts in the police and hospitals and stuff. They always seem to find out when someone's Cape starts appearing."

"The doctor must have told them about mine," Hilda said, "because my parents sent me to talk to her when I told them that I could make tiny horses appear. It wasn't a normal kind of doctor's office, though. There was carpet on the wall and very few windows. Anyway, I think she must have passed it on somehow. Mr. Souperman came to see my parents the next day."

"Yeah, I think the fire department said something about me. My parents had to call them to get me down off the roof," said Mary. "That was two years ago. Mr. Souperman said it was very early for a Cape to start working—it's normally when you're about ten."

"So," continued Hilda, "you come to The School to learn to control your Cape and practice it, develop it, so you can work out if it's good enough for you to become fully operational one day."

"Hoooo?"

Mary rolled her eyes.

Hilda, who still had some patience remaining and actually seemed to be rather enjoying Murph's turn as a confused owl, carried on: "Operational. You know? As in actually using your Cape to fight crime, catch the bad guys? They don't tell us much about it, but I bet you get a costume, a cool car, catchphrases, and **EVERYTHING!"**

"Look in here," said Mary, leading Murph into the lunchroom/auditorium, which they were just passing. Murph had been in there for lunch yesterday, but now it was deserted. "This is what it's all about." Mary was pointing upward to a stone plaque he hadn't noticed before, set into the wall above the stage.

THE HEROES' VOW
I promise to save without glory,
To help without thanks,
And to fight without fear.
I promise to keep our secrets,
Uphold our vow,
And learn what it means
To be a true Hero.

"That's the promise you make if you get to join the Heroes' Alliance," said Hilda reverently. "I knew it by heart by the end of the first day—"

"But hardly any of us get to join the real Heroes," Mary interrupted, bursting Hilda's bubble. "Mostly The School just teaches you to control your Cape so you can hide it. Only a few Capes are any good for real crime fighting, you know?" She glanced uneasily at Hilda as she said this. "Only the really great ones. The rest of us will have to try to keep them under wraps so we can have a normal life after school. Some people's Capes are really random, actually. There's a kid in the final year called Barry Talbot who can make his teeth scream. What use is that? It frightens the dentist, I suppose."

"Still, there's nothing wrong with dreaming, is there?" said Hilda determinedly. "Whether you make it or not, there's nothing wrong with wanting to be a Hero. Or designing your costume or working out what your Hero name would be. Not that I've done any of that," she added quickly, blushing.

"Okay—so most of you are here to learn how to hide your superpowers?" asked Murph, dropping his owl act for a moment. "Sorry—*Capes*. You're supposed to pretend you *don't* have a power? Well, for the first time in forty-eight hours, that sounds like something I can actually do."

Murph felt a little more optimistic after his chat with Mary and Hilda. His mind was still humming with questions, but at least he felt like he knew the basics, even if the basics could be summarized with the following words:

Secret bonkers school. No Cape. Trapped. Can't tell anyone about it.

The next day, on the other side of town, Nicholas Knox was striding through the reception area of Ribbon Robotics as if he owned the place. His hair was swept back into a greased wave, and at the end of his long legs his shiny shoes stole everyone else's light and flicked it back at them contemptuously. He had a black leather briefcase that looked very much as if it might be full of evil plans tucked under one arm.

Since Nektar had taken over, security had become much tighter. At the back of the reception area was a row of new revolving glass doors. To enter, you had to swipe your pass on a pad beside the doors, which made a slightly annoying bleep. Then you stepped inside, and the doors revolved so slowly that you were forced to inch forward on tiptoe, squeezed tight into a glass triangle. The security systems had been personally designed by Nektar himself, whose wasp-infused brain liked nothing more than causing people a bit of needless irritation at the start of their workday.

Behind the revolving doors were three elevators. The one with a bright yellow door could only be accessed by staff with top-level security clearance. It took you up to the area prowled by Nektar—the glass-walled fourth floor of the factory. Beyond that was the tall tower at the far end of the building, but only Nektar himself had access to that.

Knox swiped his security pass beside the yellow elevator and stepped inside.

"Ah, Knox," buzzed Nektar as he watched his henchperson enter the boardroom, "I like your briefcase." Then, worrying that this wasn't a particularly evil thing to say, he followed it up with a dastardly chuckle. But all this did was make him sound as if he found briefcases mildly amusing.

"Good morning, Lord Nektar," said Knox smoothly as he sat down and made himself comfortable.

Although this was only his first day as Nektar's second-in-command, it didn't appear that way. Knox gave off an air of confidence and a smell of aftershave that made Nektar's antennae twitch.

"I thought we might discuss my—sorry, *our* plans," Knox began.

"Ah yes, number two, the plans . . . ," said Nektar, greedily rubbing his hands together. "I have an incredibly evil idea."

"Go on . . . ," Knox coaxed him.

"What is the thing we hate most in the world, more than anything?" asked Nektar.

"Anyone who stands in our way," replied Knox.

"Yes, I suppose we hate them quite a lot," Nektar conceded. "But what do we really, really hate?"

There was an awkwardly long pause, as if they were in a video that kept buffering.

"Well?" snapped Nektar.

"I'm sorry, your waspishness, I assumed you were about to answer your own question," said Knox.

"I WAS about to answer my own question," said Nektar.

Nobody said anything for another ten seconds.

"PICNICS!" said Nektar finally, at the top of his voice.

"I'm so sorry," said Knox hesitantly. "It sounded like you said 'picnics.'"

"Yes. I did. PICNICS. PICNICS! PICNICS! PICNICS! PIC ... NIIIIICS! I just love ruining them. So my evil plan is this: spoil as many picnics as possible!"

As you might have realized, the wasp DNA that had become fused with Nektar's brain had begun interfering more and more with his thoughts as the months since his accident had gone by. It had started off with the need to sting people and a great love for fizzy drinks. Then later, he'd found it more and more difficult to get out of an open doorway without banging into the frame. More recently, as the wasp part of his mind had grown yet more powerful, he had started developing an all-consuming obsession with picnics, barbecues, and, indeed, outdoor dining of any kind. The thought of other people enjoying sweet treats in the sunshine filled his whole body with rage.

"Picnics?" inquired Knox gently.

"Yes, picnics. That's my first plan. Ruin all picnics. But that, Mr. Knox, is just the beginning."

Thank goodness, thought Knox to himself. *That was starting to sound a bit stupid for a moment there.* Out loud, he asked, "And so what is the next phase of the plan?"

"I want to . . ." Nektar gestured with a long, spindly finger to make Knox come closer to him. "I want to . . . GET INTO SOMEBODY'S ICE CREAM! So when they lick, I'll BE THERE! HAHAHAHAHA!"

Knox tried to respond by raising a hand, but the loony wasp was clearly on a roll.

"Not only that! I want to crawl around someone's glass when they're having a drink and creep about under a trash-can lid and then pop out when they lift it. 'HELLO!' I'd say!"

"Sir—" piped up Knox, but again to no avail.

"I want to make a papery house in someone's attic and live there ALL SUMMER and just buzz around a bit whenever someone pops up to get the suitcases."

Knox hoped Nektar was done. "Right," he said. "Of

course, my lord, all these things are achievable. I am with you one hundred percent. However, may I make a small suggestion?"

"Has it got anything to do with picnics, ice cream, trash cans, drinks, or attics?" replied Nektar.

"Indirectly, yes. Yes, it does. It involves ALL those things," said Knox.

"Tell me more, you smart-briefcased devil."

"So," said Knox, ignoring Nektar's second odd briefcase-based compliment in as many minutes, "we have mind-control helmets. We have an entire robotics factory at our disposal. We *could* attempt to take over the country."

"Oh. Why on earth would we want to do that?" whined Nektar.

"Don't you see, sir? If I—sorry, *we*—take over the country, I—I mean *us*, argh—WE then have control of . . . everything."

Nektar looked up slowly, his crispy neck clicking as he did so. "Everything?" he asked hungrily.

"Everything, sir," Knox confirmed.

"Even . . . picnics?"

"Oh yes, sir, especially picnics. Help me take over the country and you can ruin ALL picnics, forever."

"And . . . can I get in ice cream?"

"Yes."

"Trash cans?"

"Yes."

"Attics?"

"**OH, FLIPPING YES!** I mean, yes, sir. Of course, sir," said Knox, almost losing his composure. But luckily Nektar was too excited to notice. "I will re-task the robotics unit to begin construction of more mind-control helmets straight away. We have Penny Percival's spy drones all ready to deploy. I can send them out across the area looking for people to mind-control—we can pinpoint the most powerful and intelligent—and use them to begin constructing our own army."

"Excellent work, Knox!" said Nektar. "I think you're right. It's time to lure a few likely candidates into our little honey trap!"

"That's bees," sighed Knox.

"Knox, unleash the drones!" yelled Nektar dramatically.

He found that he'd really enjoyed shouting that. So much so that he said it again, even louder: "UNLEASH THE DRONES!"

Never one for subtlety, the giant wasp felt like it needed maybe one more.

"UNLEASH TH—"

Knox disagreed. "Right away, sir," he said, sweeping out of the room.

Nektar wandered over to the window to survey the streets and houses in the distance that would soon be under his control. He nodded to himself, and felt it appropriate to murmur his new catchphrase again, changing it slightly to make it seem more final.

"Yes, unleash those drones."

10

Hilda's Cape

 bellowed Mr. Flash.

Murph was three weeks into his time at The School, and the one thing he had learned conclusively was that Mr. Flash liked to start the day with a really good bellow.

For the youngest students, every day started with an hour of Capability Training, the one lesson Murph had absolutely no chance of being any good at. He was getting a little bit sick of being reminded of this fact every single morning.

"So, with the exception of Kid Normal over there, this is the part of the day where we try and hone your Capes and get you ready to play ball, so to speak." Mr. Flash seemed to think of most things in life as a game or match of some kind. "As I explained during the first week of school," he continued, "your first year at The School is the only time you'll be having CT lessons all together. In the summer, we'll be splitting you into two groups based on how useful your Cape is and how well you can control it. Separating the wheat from the chuff, as it were."

"It's 'chaff,' not 'chuff,'" said a soft voice from the side of the classroom. Murph looked across and saw that Mr. Drench was sitting there. Murph recognized him as the small man he'd seen the evening he and his mom had first encountered Mr. Souperman. He was easy to miss, sitting silently against the wall, his fluffy hair not quite hiding large, slightly pointed ears.

Mr. Flash paused, looking irritably across at his colleague. "Ah, yes, the chaff, of course. One of your specialities, Mr. Drench." Mr. Flash turned back toward the class. "By the way, Mr. Drench over here is going to share custody of you lot from now on, and then next year he'll look after those of you unable to—how shall we say?—spread the mustard. The winners will continue with me," Mr. Flash declared.

"It's 'cut the mustard,'" said Drench under his breath, unable to get a word in edgewise.

"Well, Drench, we've got quite a few candidates for

you here, so why don't you tell us what your group's all about?" Mr. Flash continued gruffly.

"Certainly," replied Mr. Drench with a fake thin-lipped smile.

He stood up, although you could barely tell. He was a mole-like man, short and stubby with rounded shoulders visible underneath his horrible tweed jacket. He pushed a pair of small, round eyeglasses farther up his nose and began speaking.

"As Mr. Flash was saying, I'll be taking most of you for CT next year. It'll be my job to make sure that once you have finished school you are able to hide your Capes as well as possible in real life. The world's a dangerous place for someone with a conspicuous or volatile Cape—there are people out there who would love to ridicule you publicly, or worse still, use your Cape for evil."

Hilda's hand shot up.

"Yes, Ms. Baker?" replied Mr. Drench.

"How will you decide which of us go in Mr. Flash's class?" she asked.

"It's quite simple. It all depends on how you perform in the P-CAT."

Murph, baffled, started to hoot, before realizing no one else apart from Mary and Hilda would get the joke. "**Whooo** . . . who can tell me what the P-CAT is, please?" he said.

"I can," said Mr. Flash, jumping to his large feet again. "The P-CAT is the Practical Capability Aptitude Test, and it happens every spring. On that day you'll be pushed to your absolute limits, and those who prevail will join the highfliers in my class. The 'remnants,' as I like to call them, will be with old Drenchy over here, learning how to hide." He spat the last word out viciously, making it very clear what he thought about the kids that ended up in Mr. Drench's class. "And that's all I'm gonna tell you about the P-CAT for now because the first rule of P-CAT is . . . if you ask me about it, I'll tell you to shut up."

Mary was feeling extra mischievous today. "Sir?" she began.

"Yes?" Mr. Flash snapped.

"About the P-CAT—"

"SHUT UP!" he barked.

Mary put her head down so Mr. Flash couldn't see her chuckling. As she looked around for an ally, Murph caught her eye and made a face. Meanwhile, Mr. Drench rolled his eyes and slid back down into his seat.

"Anyway, you little squirts, you'll find out more about that on the day. Until then, I just need to see that you're making progress in the way you control your Cape and make sure that you're able to keep it hidden from prying eyes. Right, then, who's going to go first today?"

"I will, sir," said a rather confident young man by the name of Charlie.

"Ah yes, Charlie," replied Mr. Flash, "announce your Cape to the class . . ."

"Eye-heat beams, sir."

"Right. The technical term for Charlie's Cape is, of

course, Visually Controlled Thermal Concentration, or VCTC for short." Mr. Flash squeaked the letters onto the blackboard as he spoke. "A very handy Cape this, folks. Maybe even one the Alliance might find useful if developed to a really high level. I remember a time when this Cape got them out of a sticky situation. Or, should I say, chilly situation. The Ice Fiend Invasion of '92 was no match for my old pal Doctor Thermo, who soon saw them off with a couple of stares. Great days . . . great days. Anyway. Anyone got a muffin?"

What a weird story, Murph thought. But eager as he was to hear more about the Ice Fiends, he suddenly realized that for the first time ever, he could actually contribute something to a CT lesson. Namely, a muffin. His mom had been given a baking book for her birthday, and the best consequence of this so far was the freshly baked break-time muffin she'd given Murph every morning for the past week. This was his chance.

Murph's hands shot up in the air, holding the muffin aloft like a baby lion. Although we should point out for legal reasons that it was nothing whatsoever like a scene from the film *The Lion King*.

"Chuck it over here, then, Cooper," barked Mr. Flash, reaching out and catching Murph's tossed muffin. He set it down on the center of his wooden desk.

"Let's see what you're made of, Charlie," he said. "Do your worst."

Charlie stood up. The class fell silent. He placed a finger on each temple, as if he was about to screw them into his head. He bared his teeth like the evil uncle of a noble lion prince—which, again, had nothing to do with *The Lion King*. He widened his eyes and stared intently at the muffin.

Gradually, it began to smoke.

Murph looked around. The rest of his classmates were openmouthed and expectant. Murph was just annoyed; he'd been looking forward to that muffin. It was a blueberry one.

The plume of smoke grew larger. There was a sudden loud *pop* as one of the blueberries burst in the intense heat, and then the whole thing was engulfed in flames as the paper around it caught fire. It was well and truly an ex-muffin.

"Oh dear, oh dear, how awful for you, young Cooper,"

guffawed Mr. Flash, seeing the expression on his face. "Don't look at me like that"—Murph *was* looking at him like that—**"IT'S MUFFIN TO DO WITH ME!"**

He laughed uproariously and cocked his head at a tall girl in the second row with stark white-blond hair: "Sort it out, Miss Thompson."

With a flick of her long hair, the girl got to her feet and gestured toward the flames as if to say "stop." There was a sharp crackling noise as the muffin was immediately covered in frost.

"Oh, that's really coming along, isn't it. Very nice indeed, Elsa," Mr. Flash congratulated her. "See that, everybody? True talent, the both of you. I'll certainly hope to see you in my class next year. And thank you, Cooper, for supplying the muffin. Not a complete waste of space, are you, after all? Just make sure you always bring a selection of pastries from now on."

The class all laughed. Elsa, who, we should point

out, has absolutely nothing to do with the film *Frozen*, sat back down with a smug expression. There was a tiny tinkling noise as Murph's muffin fell to the floor and smashed.

"Cheers, everyone," Murph said, deflated. And hungry.

"Right, you horrible bunch, who's next? Who haven't we heard from for a while?" asked Mr. Flash.

Out of the corner of his eye, Murph noticed a slightly plump arm waving about in the far corner of the classroom. It was Hilda.

Murph couldn't wait to see how she got on in CT with her truly unique Cape.

"Come on, then, Ms. Baker, let's get this over with," Flash said.

Hilda shuffled up to the front of the class, her cheeks glowing as she side-stepped the puddle that used to be Murph's muffin.

"Now, the Capes we've seen so far today are useful ones," said Mr. Flash, going back into lecturing mode. "Hilda, however"—he gestured at Hilda, who was hopping anxiously from foot to foot—"has, like many of you at

The School, what we describe as an 'anomalous Cape.' Or to put it another way, a completely useless one. Hilda, please demonstrate."

Murph knew what was about to happen, and he couldn't wait.

Undeterred by Flash's criticism, Hilda sprang into a sort of judo combat stance, with both her palms stretched out in front of her. She screwed her face up in concentration and, with a minuscule whinnying noise, her two tiny horses popped into being and cantered across the tabletop.

The class erupted with joy, with many students immediately grabbing their cell phones to try and take pictures. Mr. Flash rapidly regained control of the room with the internationally recognized teacher noise, which consists of going **_"ERRRRRRRR!"_** at the top of your voice.

"ERRRRRRRR!"

thundered Mr. Flash at a lung-busting volume.

The class fell silent.

Mr. Drench had risen to his feet again. "This is exactly what shouldn't happen," he told them earnestly in his reedy voice. "We must keep these Capes secret and away from prying eyes. You must NOT take photographs of Hilda's horses, or anything else you see in this classroom," he said.

"Ha!" Mr. Flash cut in. "Imagine what people would say if they saw a picture of a small, round girl producing ridiculous small horses willy-nilly."

Hilda's lower lip began to quiver.

"They'd lock her up for being a loony!" he roared. "They'd call her a freak! A small, round, horse-producing freak! And they'd be right. That's what she is!"

Hilda burst into tears and fled back to her desk, the horses vanishing into thin air with the tiniest of neighs.

"And that," continued Mr. Flash, "is why Hilda, and most of the rest of you, need to learn to control your Capes. Not so you can use them, but so you can conceal them. Hilda can live a normal life as long as she doesn't go producing horses from her hands every time she gets a bit excited!"

Thankfully, at that moment the bell rang, signifying the end of this onslaught for poor Hilda. Most of the class gathered up their things and disappeared into the hallway. But Murph and Mary packed up deliberately slowly so they would be the last to leave. When the classroom had emptied, they shuffled over to Hilda, who was sitting there with a glum face.

"Don't worry about Flash," said Murph, putting his hand on her shoulder. "I LOVE your tiny horses. He's just being nasty. And he wasted a good muffin."

"Yeah, he's a big bully. Don't pay them any mind. Be proud of your Cape," Mary chimed in. "It makes you who you are."

Hilda looked up. Her face was wet with tears, and her

nose had been doing a really impressive amount of running at the same time. She wiped her arm across her face, smearing everything into one blob of wet, post-cry slime.

"Thanks, guys," said Hilda, or, as she had briefly become, the Snot Monster. "I think it's the best Cape around. Mr. Flash doesn't know what he's talking about."

"I agree," Murph reassured her.

Hilda smiled. Mary and Murph helped her pack up her bag and gave her a tissue before stopping to clear up two tiny-horse "presents" that had been left on the desk.

"Right!" said Murph. "Who wants ice cream?"

"Great idea," said Mary.

"And a new muffin for Murph!" joked Hilda.

"Yeah, and a new muffin. Stupid Mr. Flash," he replied.

And for the first time in months, Murph found himself actually laughing as they walked off down the hall in search of treats.

11

The Posse

"I'm home!" Murph called out, still in fine spirits as he let himself into the ugly new house. But even its ugly newness wasn't getting to him today. He threw his bag down in the hall and wandered around looking for someone to share his mood with. He thought he could hear his mom's voice coming from the kitchen, and as he got closer he realized she was on the phone.

"I just want some kind of guarantee that you're going to be able to keep me on after next summer is all . . ." he heard her say.

Murph's spirit dropped at least five notches on the spirit scale (it's out of ten by the way and had been nudging a good seven). He hated these conversations and recognized them immediately. It was an "I want to make absolutely sure we're not going to have to move again" sort of conversation, and he'd become depressingly familiar with them over the past three years. He was also familiar with his mom's various acting techniques as she tried to disguise what was going on and make everything seem okay. Sadly, in terms of acting ability, she was about as natural as Astroturf.

"But I thought things were going we—" She cut herself off as she noticed Murph hovering in the kitchen doorway like a novice ghost. "Look, we'll talk more next week, just please do what you can. Okay, thanks, Ben, bye." She put the phone down and ushered Murph in for a hug.

"That was work, right?" said Murph. "Didn't sound great."

"We'll sort it out," his mom reassured him.

Murph suddenly remembered what Flora had said to him, and it felt appropriate to repeat it. "These things have a way of coming out in the wash."

"I suppose they do," she sighed and hugged him tighter.

Despite these encouraging words, Murph's spirit scale didn't get beyond a wobbly five that evening. He decided to cheer himself up with a pre-bedtime treat and some alone time, so he wandered out of the house toward the row of small shops nearby. It was getting late now and they were mostly closed. Murph squinted up into the chilly, sleety drizzle that had begun to fall and stuffed his hands deeper into his pockets. He was just about to make a dash for the warm, inviting windows of the one shop that was open, Mickey's News, when something caught his eye from the triangular patch of grass across the street.

It was a tiny, winking green light. And he'd seen it before.

As you may have noticed, Murph is an inquisitive kid. Mysterious green lights, unexpected popping sounds, strangely colored liquids, or birds with the power of speech: none of these things will go uninvestigated if Murph's around. So he casually crossed the road, leaving the circle of streetlight to move cautiously onto the damp grass and pick his way between some pale, unimpressive trees.

The tiny, bright light was beaming from a bench near a bus stop on the main road. There were two people sitting on it, chatting to each other in low voices. Murph watched as a green shaft of light lit up the girl's pocket.

She slapped her hand to it instantly and pulled out a phone.

"Posse receiving," she said. Murph slowly realized who they were. It was the pair who'd directed him to Mr. Souperman's office: Deborah, the tall girl with the dark hair, and beside her, Dirk, the cool-looking boy in the blazer.

Posse receiving? thought Murph. It was an odd way to answer your phone. What on earth was wrong with a standard "Hello"?

But the girl had started speaking again.

"Cowgirl active. The Sheriff active. Ready to respond. Over." Deborah was plugging a wireless earpiece into her ear with her other hand. She listened intently, then nodded: **"Accepted. Posse active and responding. Let's move."**

The last two words were directed at Dirk, and without a second's hesitation they both got up from the bench and sprinted away, the spray from their shoes making a mist behind them on the wet street.

Without thinking, Murph darted across the road after them. Whatever was going on, he wanted a look at it. Thirty seconds later and he'd have been flattened by a bus, but luckily for him this isn't that sort of story.

The pair was already well ahead of him, but Murph put on a burst of speed and was just in time to see them take a right into a side road. Murph cranked his pace up as far as it would go. Like a cheetah with its back legs on fire, he pelted toward the corner, and by a nanosecond he was in time to catch a glimpse of their silhouetted figures going right again into an alleyway some distance down the narrow road.

By now Murph's lungs felt as though they had been pumped full of hot sand. He leaned against a lamppost on the corner of the side street, heart twanging like a demented ukulele, and concentrated on doing some really high-quality panting for twenty full seconds.

When Murph regained the use of his legs, he walked cautiously down the road. There were strange noises coming from the alley. There was a clang as if a garbage can had been knocked over, followed by shouted words he couldn't quite make out.

Suddenly, someone came dashing out of the alley. It was a man, and he was running as fast as he could.

Murph was too shocked to do anything—he gazed openmouthed as the man bore down on him, legs pumping like pistons. He was carrying an expensive-looking leather handbag in one hand, which, though lovely, didn't quite blend with the sneakers, jeans, and blue T-shirt he was wearing. If he hadn't stolen the bag it would have been a crime against fashion. As he *had*, in fact, stolen the bag, it was just a crime.

Behind the thief, Murph saw the silhouette of Deborah Lamington as she stepped out into the street, holding something large and round.

"Stop him!" she yelled.

Startled, Murph glanced behind him to see who she was talking to. By the time he looked back, the man was upon him. He shoved Murph roughly out of the way, knocking him into the wet road between two parked cars.

Murph heard the man's running footsteps recede down the street, and then there was another trash can–like clang and everything fell silent.

Exhausted, bruised, and scared, Murph had just made the decision to lie a little longer in the nice, comfortable oily puddle he'd discovered, when someone spoke to him:

"Are you okay?"

"Yeah, I think so," said Murph, slightly embarrassed that he'd chickened out, then been knocked over like an ineffectual bowling pin.

Deborah—or Cowgirl as she seemed to call herself in this kind of situation—had appeared in the gap between the cars. She held out her hand to haul him up.

"Who's this?" said another voice. It was Dirk—he'd arrived seemingly out of nowhere, very quickly, much to Murph's surprise.

"It's that kid from school, the one we directed to Souperman," replied Cowgirl. She turned back to Murph. "You could have at least tried to give me an assist. Or are you one of Mr. Drench's lot—the hiders?"

"Meeeerm . . . ," started Murph, brushing the front of his jeans casually, as if that would help remove the gallon of oily water that had soaked into the back of them.

"Hang on, I know who it is," said the boy suddenly. "It's that new kid! The one with no Cape . . . Kid—"

"Normal, yeah," said Murph gloomily.

"I'm Debs," said Deborah Lamington, "Cowgirl when I'm operational."

"Right," hedged Murph, "and . . . the Sheriff, right?"

"How did you know his code name?" asked Deborah. "Did one of the older kids at school tell you? Or did you hear me on the HALO unit?"

"The, uh, HALO unit, yeah. Right."

"Well, we'd better call this one in," continued Deborah/Debs/Cowgirl.

She produced the smooth black handset again and spoke into it. **"Posse transmitting . . . Suspect neutralized . . . Repeat that? . . . En route now? . . . Understood. We'll clear."** She turned to Dirk. "We've got police on the way. Better secure Mr. Mugger over there."

With a jerk of her head, she motioned up the road and, jolted, Murph saw the man who'd been running away lying unconscious on the sidewalk. He trailed after the other two as they headed toward the dark shape on the ground.

As he got closer, he spotted an old-fashioned metal trash-can lid on the floor beside the man's head.

Deborah picked it up, spun on her heel in just about the coolest way you can imagine, and threw it back down the road like a Frisbee. It skimmed above the cars, turned an elegant corner, and disappeared into the alleyway, where there was a loud *bedoinggg* noise, followed by clattering. It was the exact sound a metal trash-can lid makes when it comes to rest on top of a metal trash can. Pop outside and have a try if you want to know what it sounds like, and you have really retro trash cans.

Deborah then produced a length of rope that had been wound around her waist like a belt and flicked it toward the unconscious man. It seemed to animate itself like a snake, tying his hands and feet securely together.

Murph was beginning to think that Deborah Lamington was kind of awesome. She picked up the handbag and handed it to the Sheriff, raising her eyebrows.

"I'm on it," he declared, before following this up with dramatic mouth-trumpet fan fare. Deborah rolled her eyes as he started to run down the road, blurred, and vanished.

"Whoa!" marveled Murph. "He's got the same Cape as Mr. Flash, only faster!"

"Don't let Flash hear you say that," warned Deborah. "Now, you get out of here. I've got to deal with these people." Blue lights were reflecting off her face as a police car pulled up. "And listen," she continued, "don't follow us again, okay? This isn't a game, and it certainly isn't safe for someone like you."

Murph's stomach felt like it had hit the floor and rolled around in something stinky. For a minute there he'd almost been able to kid himself that he was on a mission with a pair of real superheroes. But Deborah's words had made the reality of it clear; he'd creepily followed them, been too cowardly to help when they needed it, and now he was being told to scram.

Without another word Murph turned and wandered

away down the street. As he reached the corner he looked back to see Deborah showing some kind of identity card in a leather wallet to two police officers. "Refer it to CAMU," he overheard her saying. But he was too miserable to wonder what that meant, or to stay and find out.

Murph spent a few days kicking himself for not sticking a foot out and tripping up the mugger. But it's never a good idea to spend too long kicking yourself—you just get a sore bottom and end up falling over. In the end he decided that even if he had tripped him up, it wouldn't have done much good. What was he expecting? It wasn't as if the pair was suddenly going to ask him to join their crime-fighting gang, which seemed to be called the Posse. What was he going to be alongside Cowgirl and the Sheriff? The Amazing Trip Boy? Captain Ankle?

But the sight of two real-life Heroes in action had got him itching to find out more about the Alliance, even if it meant resorting to extreme measures, like speaking to Mr. Flash.

"Sir," began Murph toward the end of a CT lesson a few days later. A gangly kid from the front row had just been demonstrating his Cape, the ability to communicate with cats. But the cat that the janitor had brought in on a cart hadn't seemed especially interested. Eventually it had just curled up and gone to sleep.

"Yes, Kid Normal?" replied Mr. Flash, never missing an opportunity to rub Murph's nose in his own nickname.

"How do you join the Heroes' Alliance?" he asked boldly.

"Nothing you ever need to worry about, Cooper," said Mr. Flash dismissively, but the question had got the rest of the class excited.

"Oh, come on, sir, please, yes, tell us about becoming a Hero," begged Hilda from the other side of the room.

"Nobody calls them Heroes anymore, horsey," snapped Mr. Flash, but his eyes glinted. Murph realized he'd hit on a subject Mr. Flash loved talking about.

"Well, the Heroes' Alliance, as I explained to most of you in your first week here, is an organization that ninety-nine percent of you will never be asked to join. It was originally formed over thirty years ago to combat . . ." He stopped himself briefly, then continued, "Well, you don't need to know exactly why it was formed.

But these days it coordinates the activities of a small number of secret operatives who assist our normal law enforcement agencies when needed. Alliance operatives are highly trained, highly skilled—and their activities are kept top secret. So you can forget any silly ideas you might have gotten from comics about flying about town in plain sight or wearing some oddball costume."

Hilda looked a little crestfallen. "But I thought Heroes used to wear costumes," she said in a small voice. Mr. Flash flashed over to her desk and loomed above her like a bald cloud.

"They USED to wear costumes? Of course they *used* to, back in the day. Before any interfering dimwit with a video camera could blow your whole secret identity in seconds! And don't even get me started on the blasted internet." He whooshed back to his desk and continued muttering something angry-sounding about "twits and face pages."

"They must have been great days, I bet, eh, Mr. Flash?" asked Mary, glancing across and smiling at Murph. If they played this right, the rest of the period could easily be taken up with the teacher's reminiscences.

"Indeed they were, Ms. Perkins," said Mr. Flash, going a bit dewy-eyed at the thought. "Genuine Heroes, with genuine costumes, sidekicks, you name it. Even you might have stood a chance back in the day, with your little yellow umbrella." He looked at her almost sentimentally, but Mary bristled.

"What's wrong with my umbrella?"

"What's wrong with it? You can't fly without it, that's what's wrong with it! Craziest thing I've seen in thirty years teaching here." Murph looked across at Mary with interest. He'd always assumed her umbrella was just part of her unique fashion sense.

She was blushing. "Well, it's not my fault I can't skim without it."

Mr. Flash made a dismissive snorting noise. "Wouldn't be much good on a real mission though, would ya?" he taunted. "What happens if you lost your 'brella, eh? You'd be as much use as a solar-powered owl!"

Murph decided to try and get the conversation back to what Mr. Flash had referred to as the "Golden Age" to save Mary any further embarrassment. "Tell us about some of the old Heroes, then, sir," he prompted him.

"Oooh, yes, please, Mr. Flash," pleaded Hilda. "Tell us about a Hero from this town."

"None of the really cool Heroes would have come from this town," countered Charlie, the eye-heat-beams boy. "They all would have operated out of the big cities."

"This town? *This town?* **THIS TOWN IS ONE OF THE MOST FAMOUS IN THE WHOLE ANNALS OF CAPABILITY!**" spluttered Mr. Flash, who seemed as insulted as if Charlie had made an unkind comment about the size of his mother's bottom. "This town was rumored to be the home base of the most celebrated and mysterious Hero of them all, I'll have you know!"

The whole class was now desperate to know more: "Who was that, sir? Tell us about him! Tell us, Mr. Flash, **pleeeeease!**"

"All right, all right," said Mr. Flash, seating himself in the internationally recognized teacher storytelling pose: standing half upright with his military-fatigued behind braced against his desk.

He proceeded to tell them a story about the most

powerful and most mysterious of all the Heroes of the Golden Age, a figure not seen for more than thirty years, who disappeared into the shadows as suddenly as they had once appeared.

12

The Legend of the
Blue Phantom

1965

It was the middle of the decade nicknamed the "Swinging Sixties" because of the large number of new playgrounds that were built around that time. As usual, Great Britain's most suave and famous secret agent, James James, was taking a long lunch.

He sidled up to the bar at his favorite restaurant and beckoned the white-jacketed, brown-mustached bartender over with a casual wave of his left eyebrow.

"Chocolate milkshake, please, Gaston," he drawled.

"Shaken or stirred, sir?" asked Gaston.

James James was thrown slightly by this, but he didn't let it show. "Stirred, please," he demanded confidently.

The bartender turned his back for a moment, then presented to him a glass of milk with all the chocolate syrup sunk to the bottom.

James James thought for a moment. "Now shake it, please, Gaston," he demanded. "A chocolate milkshake, stirred . . . then shaken."

Gaston poured the milkshake into a shaker and shook it, which, as the name "milkshake" implies, is what you're supposed to do.

But the super-spy failed to notice this, as his attention had been diverted by the woman next to him at the bar. She was wearing a long evening dress, even though it was only long lunchtime, and had wavy dark hair that hid half her face in exactly the way secret agents really, really like.

The spy slid down the bar so he was a bit closer to her, stumbling slightly at the halfway point.

"Well, hello there. The name's James. James James," he oozed.

The woman turned to face him with a puzzled expression. "James James James?" she queried.

"No, not James James James, just James James.

But please"—he raised his more powerful right eyebrow—"don't let's be formal. Call me James."

"I'm Jane. Jane Jane," said the woman, flicking her hair back over her shoulder like she was in a shampoo commercial.

"Really?" asked James James.

"No, not really. That would be ridiculous," she replied. "Jane Smith."

James James had rather hoped her name would be something more like Slinky McSpy; he was a big fan of a novelty name on a lady. But he didn't let his disappointment show. Instead, he took a long sip on his drink through a stripy straw.

He gagged.

"Aargh! Gaston, this hot chocolate is stone cold!"

"It's a *milkshake*, sir," replied Gaston coolly. "And there's a telephone call for you."

He handed James James an old-fashioned black phone on a silver tray, although the phone didn't look old-fashioned to any of them because it was the 1960s. They thought it looked really quite up-to-date, even

though it was plugged into the wall with a wire, which made carting it around on a tray very inconvenient.

James picked up the receiver, thinking to himself how marvelous modern technology was.

"James?" said a voice at the other end, which he recognized as Em, the head of the Secret Service. It was short for Emma.

"Please, sir, there's no need to be so formal. Do call me James," began James James.

"Shut up, and stop calling me 'sir,'" Em snapped. She was in a rush and had no time to banter with idiots.

Neither did Jane Smith, who took this opportunity to sneak away and later enjoyed a long and successful career as an award-winning architect. But that's another, more architecture-based story.

"It's Doctor Nuke, James," continued Em. "He's planted a nuclear bomb underneath London and he's threatening to detonate it unless we pay him ten million guineas, five shillings, and seven pence ha'penny. And a farthing." (Money back then used to be more confusing.) "We've tracked him to the crypt at St. Paul's Cathedral. Hurry, James!"

"Don't worry, sir, I'm on my way to save Great Britain," shouted James James into the phone unnecessarily loudly, causing some diners in the restaurant to look up irritably from their plates of boiled liver. (Food back then wasn't great either.)

After only a five-minute pause, in which he tried to work out how much a farthing was worth, the world's greatest secret agent dashed out of the door and down the stairs to his car. He then dashed back up the stairs and picked up his car keys before dashing back down again, unlocking his car, and getting in.

Gaston finished off the milkshake.

You may already know what St. Paul's Cathedral looks like. If you don't, then please draw a picture of what you imagine it might look like and send it to us. We could do with a laugh.

In any case, whatever it looks like in your head, James James pulled up outside it in his silver sports car and rushed to the door marked "Crypt." There was a door next to it marked "Bathroom," which he was quite tempted by after his long lunch, but there was no time.

Save the world first; pee later, thought James James, remembering page one of the *Spy Handbook*.

He eased open the first door and crept softly down the stairs like a stealthy panther wearing a suit because it was on its way to the Panther of the Year awards.

At the bottom of the stairs, the secret agent eased open the door and slipped inside. He found himself in a large, chilly stone room. It was lit by gas lamps on the wall. Stone coffins were arranged in rows across the paved floor. Toward the center of the room was a large metal box, and a man with a bald head was standing at it with his back to James James, fiddling with the controls.

The spy grinned to himself—this was going to be easy.

He stepped quietly forward, and tripped over a large white cat that made a noise like a cat that had been tripped over.

The bald man ceased his fiddling and spoke without turning around: "I've been expecting you."

"Have you?" answered James James before he could stop himself.

"Yes, one margarita with extra cheese and garlic knots. Seven half crowns and four tuppence threp'ny, isn't it? I've got the money here somewhere . . ." He started to rummage in the pocket of his gray villain suit.

"I'm not the pizza guy, Doctor Nuke, this is 1965," the spy interrupted him. "It's me, James James, the world's greatest secret agent, here to put a stop to your evil schemes." Immediately he regretted saying this—his cover was blown.

Doctor Nuke slowly turned around. His face was marked by a hideous scar that ran from his left eye all the way down his cheek. He'd drawn it there in pen to look more dastardly.

"Stop my evil schemes? I don't think so." Doctor Nuke chuckled, and before James James could move, the villain had whipped out a gun and pointed it straight at James's handsome, chiseled face.

There was a moment's silence, broken only by the distant sound of the cat limping around and saying bad words in cat language.

"What happens now, then?" James James wanted to know.

"What do you mean, what happens now?" snapped Doctor Nuke. "I'm going to shoot you in the face, then get on with my plan to blow up London with this nuclear bomb. What did you expect to happen?"

"Well, I thought there'd be dinner," said the secret agent lamely.

"Dinner?"

"Yes, usually villains give me dinner, you know. Then they tell me their evil plans and tie me up and leave me unguarded, so I can escape using the fork I concealed in my sleeve while they served the chicken."

"Well," chuckled Doctor Nuke, "tough nuggets Mr. James James," which wasn't bad considering he thought of it on the spot. And he pulled the trigger . . .

There was a bang and flash from the muzzle of the gun.

But James was surprised and delighted to discover that he wasn't dead. The bullet seemed to have hit an invisible wall in the air halfway between the two men. It tinkled harmlessly to the ground.

"Looks like it's tough nuggets for you, Doctor Nuke,"

drawled James James. Then he squinted: he thought he could see some kind of disturbance in the space where the bullet had stopped—a bluish person-shaped haze. It was see-through and indistinct.

"That's my joke. You can't just steal my lines and say them back at me," raged Doctor Nuke. "Just for that, I'm going to blow up London anyway."

He turned back to his bomb, and on a control panel saying "Blow Up London" he flicked the switch to On. A display lit up, and numbers started counting down from **TEN.**

Doctor Nuke threw himself at James James and knocked him over backward.

NINE.

The two men wrestled on the floor, making grunting noises.

EIGHT.

"Your name's quite a coincidence, isn't it?" mused James James from the crook of Doctor Nuke's elbow.

SEVEN.

"How do you mean?" asked the supervillain, digging his knee into the spy's back.

SIX.

"Well, you're called Doctor Nuke," said James James, hitting him over the head with a wooden chair, "and you try to blow things up with nuclear bombs."

FIVE.

"Do you know, I'd never even thought of it like that," said Doctor Nuke, leaping from the edge of the battle arena onto the secret agent's back and clinging on as he thrashed around.

FOUR.

"I mean, imagine if you'd have been called Doctor Tortoise," laughed James James, hooking his fingers into the doctor's nostrils.

THREE.

"I'd never get anywhere fast, would I? Ahahahaha," guffawed Doctor Nuke.

TWO.

"But instead," Doctor Nuke went on, "I'm about to wipe out London with a huge devastating explosion in about one second. Ahahahahahaha . . ."

ONE.

Click.

Nothing exploded.

Both men stopped their wrestling—which they had actually just been starting to really enjoy—got to their feet, and turned to the bomb. The bluish outline of . . . someone . . . could now be seen beside the control panel, hand outstretched to the control switch, which had just been flicked to Off.

As they watched, the figure solidified into the shape of a person in a blue costume. Its face was hidden behind a silvery-blue helmet and its torso protected by armor in the same color.

"That armor's bulletproof," realized James James, and whistled in admiration. "And you can go invisible."

The helmeted figure nodded.

"You got between me and the gun," he marveled.

The figure nodded silently once again, then looked sharply to the right. Doctor Nuke was making a run for the door.

Like a total legend, the blue-clad Hero leaped athletically over the nearest stone coffin, turned a perfect somersault in midair, and brought the bad guy

to the ground with a flying scissor kick. Doctor Nuke's head hit the stone floor with an extremely satisfying noise, knocking him out cold.

His silvery-blue attacker, still crouched in a combat stance, looked back at James James expectantly. Not sure what to do, the spy gave a thumbs-up sign and a slight nod, as if to say: "Well done on taking down Doctor Nuke with that awesome display of hand-to-hand combat, but I actually had the situation perfectly under control."

The mysterious figure gestured impatiently to Doctor Nuke, who was now snoring like a drunken sea lion, then pointed toward the door that led to the stairs.

"Ah yes, quite right, let's get him outside," said James James. "It's time for Doctor Nuke to have a long stretch of, um, doctor's surgery . . . in prison."

He'd been trying for a pithy one-liner but had fallen woefully short. Instead he'd talked total gibberish for two precious seconds. His silvery-blue rescuer indicated this with a pitying wiggle of the hands, then helped him carry the limp form of Doctor Nuke up the stairs.

As they burst into the fresh air, James James gasped. Parked beside his silver sports car was a vehicle that quite frankly made everything else within a two-mile radius, including the cathedral, look trashy.

It was made of gleaming polished chrome. Its long, delicately curved hood led up to an airplane-style cockpit. Behind that, stretching across the top of the fuselage and supported by metal struts, was a single silver wing. Huge, polished black tires shone at each corner. And on either side of it, just behind the doors, were two long, thin jet engines.

James James looked at his own car, of which he was unreasonably proud, and realized that compared to this vehicle it might as well have been a cardboard box with "car" written on the side in crayon.

The door of the beautiful contraption opened, and the silvery-blue Hero who had just rescued him from certain death darted over to it and disappeared inside. Just before the door closed, a gloved hand reached out and flicked out a small white card.

With a roar, its jets started up and the machine rose swiftly into the air. It hovered there for a moment, and then, just when you thought it couldn't get any more awesome, the engines swiveled smoothly so they were pointing backward, and the vehicle disappeared above the cathedral's roof, leaving a faint, curved vapor trail of different shades of blue in the cool early evening air.

James James walked over to the scorched patch of road where the incredible vehicle had rested and picked up the card. As police sirens grew louder he turned it over and read, in neat, cursive handwriting:

You just got saved by
The Blue Phantom

13

The Captain and the Weasel

For the rest of the semester, Murph and his friends tried everything they could think of to persuade Mr. Flash to tell them more about the mysterious Blue Phantom. Hilda seemed especially fascinated. "What was his armor like?" she asked Mr. Flash the next day. But he pretended he hadn't heard her. She tried again a few times, but eventually he roared directly into her face, "You've had your little history lesson. Now get on with some work!" He seemed, if anything, a little embarrassed that he'd allowed himself to get so caught up in his reminiscences.

The Christmas break passed fairly uneventfully for Murph, if you didn't count all the jokes from Andy about his secret school. Apparently they were never going to stop being funny.

"Is there a Yule Ball in the Great Hall, Smurph Face?" he'd asked every day, pirouetting around the kitchen. "Will you daaaaaaance with Professor McGonagall?"

The other notable thing about winter that year was the unusual number of wasps. The local newspaper had run a story about it before Christmas, under the headline **BUZZ-CEMBER,** which was not especially clever on any level.

In the article, which Murph read over breakfast one morning, they quoted a pest control expert who said he'd never been called out to so many wasp sightings in winter before, and that the wasps seemed to be of unusual size and totally impossible to catch. One old lady rang up the local radio station, trying to insist that they weren't actually wasps but robots sent to spy on her. The presenters just laughed and played another song.

It was on their first day back—an iron-gray January afternoon—that the subject of the Blue Phantom was raised again. As Murph walked toward the first CT lesson of the New Year, he ran into Hilda, who had clearly been doing a lot of thinking over the break.

"I mean," she puffed, trotting alongside him, "I don't

understand what happened. If, years ago, there used to be real superheroes . . ."

"Yes?" Murph prompted her.

"Then . . . why aren't there superheroes anymore?" asked Hilda.

"Well, there are," replied Murph, stopping to think. "But they're, you know, secret now. No more costumes, like Mr. Flash said."

"Well, it's a shame about the costumes," sulked Hilda. "I think a real Hero should have a costume. If I make it into the Heroes' Alliance I'm totally having one. And what happened to the Blue Phantom? He was the coolest of them all. What if he's still out there somewhere? Just waiting to swoop in and rescue people?"

"Wouldn't the Blue Phantom be, like, eighty years old or something by now?" Murph reasoned. "He's not going to be swooping anywhere at that age."

But Hilda clearly had a bee in her bonnet about this. Mr. Drench was taking them for CT that morning, and as soon as the class began to settle down, her arm was waving in the air.

"Yes, Ms. Baker?" said Mr. Drench in a bored voice,

folding up a newspaper and stuffing it into the pocket of his tweed jacket.

"If there used to be superheroes," asked Hilda stridently, "why aren't there real superheroes any more?"

Mr. Drench screwed his face up. "What on earth do you mean, 'real Heroes'?"

"You know." Hilda was on a roll. "Real ones with costumes, like the Blue Phantom? You know about him, don't you?"

"Of course," the teacher replied slightly reluctantly.

"Aha! Well, what happened to him, then?" asked Hilda triumphantly. "Did he die? What was his costume made of? No, don't worry about the costume for now. But what happened to him? What was his catchphrase? No, don't worry about that either."

Mr. Drench paused and glanced around at the expectant class, looking a little like a sleepy zoo animal surrounded by wide-eyed onlookers.

With his inquisitive mind whizzing, Murph forced the issue.

"Why was the Blue Phantom the greatest, Mr. Drench?" he asked.

The teacher sighed, trapped. "Look. Let's just say that the Blue Phantom was . . . different. A hero for heroes. The sort of character who saved the people normally doing the saving."

There was a pause.

Murph, at the back of class, got an inkling that there was more of a story here. "Did he save you?" he asked quietly.

Mr. Drench looked even more uncomfortable. "Well," he said, finally, "you could put it like that."

"How? When?" asked Hilda and more or less everyone else.

"When else?" replied Mr. Drench simply. "When all hope was gone." He sat down, looking thoughtful and serious.

"I haven't always just been Mr. Drench the CT teacher, you know," he began. "We've all got a past. The day I first met the Phantom was also the first day I came into contact with the most dangerous enemy of them all. A day I wish to forget. The day I lost . . ." He trailed off.

"Lost what?" breathed Hilda eventually.

"The day I lost . . . everything," said Mr. Drench dejectedly, "and the day I realized the true role of the sidekick. Tough job being a sidekick, you know. People don't understand the sacrifice. Certainly not Captain Alpha, anyway."

"Who's Captain Alpha?" asked Hilda, hardly daring to believe they were finding out so much.

Murph suddenly remembered when he'd first met Mr. Drench, and something else clicked into place in his brain. "It's Souperman!" he exclaimed.

Mr. Drench raised his eyebrows in surprise. He seemed slightly annoyed with himself for giving the game away. "Yes, he was Captain Alpha, the strongest man on this or any planet. And I, well, I was known as the Weasel."

"Weasel?" asked Hilda incredulously.

"Yes, Weasel," he said defensively. "Weasels are actually fascinating animals. They're, um, very wily. And cunning."

"That's foxes."

"No, it's definitely weasels. And they have astonishing hearing, which is, of course, my own Capability.

Although my hearing has never been quite as exceptional since that day."

"So that's what you lost?" Murph wanted to know. "You lost your . . . Cape?"

"Part of it," said the Artist Formerly Known as the Weasel sadly. "That's what happened to anyone who came up against . . . him. Luckily, the Blue Phantom saved me before my whole Capability could be stolen."

"Did Captain Alpha lose part of his power, too?" Hilda asked in a hushed voice.

"Oh no," said Mr. Drench. "We'd split up, and I was the one who encountered our enemy first. But maybe I was thought to be the expendable one. Not all Capabilities are considered equal, as you are no doubt learning from Mr. Flash. It's certainly a lesson I learned that day."

Mr. Drench fidgeted. A few beads of sweat had appeared on his brow; clearly he was uncomfortable talking about this subject.

"Let's leave that discussion there, shall we?" he asked, eyes flitting around nervously. "What's done is done—and there is no point going over old ground.

But that's what happened: it was I who was sent in alone to face Magpie." He'd definitely said too much this time.

"Magpie? Who on earth is that?" said Murph.

"The worst nightmare of everyone in this room, apart from you, Mr. Cooper," replied the teacher drily. "But not the subject of this lesson, I'm afraid." The class let out a groan of protest as he turned and began to write on the blackboard. "Today we'll continue our discussion of how to prevent accidental Cape activation."

His head full of questions, Murph wandered along to the auditorium by himself later. As he entered, he looked up at the stone tablet bearing the Heroes' Vow, realizing the world of Heroes was bigger and more sinister than he had imagined. And how much more there was to fear. For the first time, it struck him that a world of superheroes brings with it the possibility of a world of supervillains.

Murph shuffled forward in the lunch line toward whatever delights awaited him. As he was quite short, he could only see the steam rising off the serving trays but was aware of the frantic motioning of the lunch ladies as they slopped and splatted the food onto the plates like robots on a production line. *Friendly robots though*, Murph thought. *Robots called Edna, with hairnets.* He patiently waited his turn as he edged toward the front of the line.

Suddenly it turned into a very good day. It was his favorite: spaghetti and meatballs with garlic bread. And even better than that, it was a fresh batch.

We all know what a great feeling it is watching the poor sucker before you get the scrapings from the tired, burned dish and then seeing the new one sliding into place. Murph was first in line. The new dish was ALL HIS. It's the lunchtime equivalent of getting into bed and realizing there are clean sheets—except in this case, the sheets were covered in delicious tomato sauce, with cheese pillows.

Murph was moments away from watching the spoon make its first trip into the glistening meat-fest when a sharp push to his ribs knocked him backward. The people behind him in the line grumbled as he staggered into them.

Murph looked around in confusion—it appeared that

no one had touched him—and by the time he turned back there was someone else being served the aforementioned glistening meat-fest. It was a tall, gangly, pimply kid with a wispy mustache that hung above his lip like it was embarrassed to be there.

"Oops. Did you fall over?" he asked sarcastically.

"Hey, you pushed in and . . . pushed me . . . I think," replied a confused Murph.

The mustached boy just laughed, grabbed the last three slices of garlic bread, and strolled off.

Murph was so aghast at the whole situation that he hadn't realized that the rest of the line had since swarmed past him to collect their food. The line now snaked right back to the door and he was no longer in it.

This was unfair, and Murph hated injustice. Besides, lunch was the only thing he'd been looking forward to that day. Thanks to growing up with a smelly big brother, he wasn't afraid of sticking up for himself. So he started to march over to where the gangly line-jumper had sat down and was about to address him when he noticed who was sitting at the table with him.

The boy was surrounded by what can only be

described as a terrifying collection of teenage monsters. Murph quickly nicknamed them all in his head to try and keep calm. Alongside Gangly Fuzz Face were Pork Belly Pig Breath, Corned Beef Boy, Crazy Eyes Jemima, and, last but not least, Frankenstein's Nephew. It was a shame, he thought, that these names would never see the light of day, but it was probably safer that way.

At this point, Murph realized he'd been standing there staring at this array of beasts and naming them silently for around ninety seconds. They'd all stopped chewing and were staring back at him.

Except for Jemima. You were never quite sure what she was looking at.

"WHAAAAAT?" screamed Jemima suddenly and at the top of her voice.

"He pushed me out of the way and took my place in the line," Murph replied.

"AND?" grunted Corned Beef Boy. "What you gonna do about it?"

Murph started feeling a bit worried.

"Hang on . . . Isn't this the kid with no Cape?" said one of the goons.

"Why are you even at this school anyway?" said another.

"Yeah, shove off!" laughed Gangly Fuzz Face, and once again Murph felt a powerful shove in the center of his chest. He instantly recoiled, stumbling back uncontrollably into a huge pile of dirty plates. The plates hesitated for a moment, tottered playfully from side to side, and then decided to make a nuisance of themselves and cascade everywhere.

They fell backward, showering the table behind, where, to his horror, Murph could see the bald head and broad back of Mr. Flash. A bald head and broad back that were now covered in splotches of tomato sauce and hoops of spaghetti.

Gangly Fuzz Face and his friends all scattered, terrified of being connected to what had happened. Mr. Flash got to his feet and turned around slowly, like one of those ballerinas in a music box only without the frilly skirt. His face was red, and not just because there was a significant amount of tomato sauce dripping down it like savory magma from an erupting volcano. He picked a morsel of chewed garlic bread from his mustache and surveyed the scene.

It didn't look good for Murph, who was standing right beside the smashed pile of plates.

"DID YOU DO THAT, COOPER?" shouted Mr. Flash.

Murph considered several possible answers to this question. But he only got as far as "Ummmmmm" before Mr. Flash had identified another possible culprit.

"OR WAS IT YOU, YOU GREAT LIABILITY?" he roared over Murph's shoulder.

Murph spun around and saw the boy from his class who could inflate different parts of his body. The kid looked absolutely terrified at being shouted at by a tomato-flavored monster like this, and in his panic one of his hands suddenly ballooned, sending his glass of milk flying.

This did nothing to calm down Mr. Flash. *"IT WAS YOU, WASN'T IT? YOU CLUMSY LITTLE ... YOU'VE BALLOONED ALL THE BLINKIN' PLATES OVER, HAVEN'T YOU?"*

The boy made a small whimpering noise and edged along the bench as if trying to escape, one of his ears inflating with a high-pitched whining sound.

"Problem, Mr. Flash?" said a voice.

Murph spun around again and was relieved to see Flora, the old lady who sat outside the headmaster's office, carrying a cup of tea.

"You seem to be covered in bolognese," she went on helpfully. "We should go and get you cleaned up."

Mr. Flash made a spluttering noise and flicked a meatball off his shoulder.

"Come along," continued Flora brightly, and she led him away firmly by the arm, but not before turning to Murph with a wink.

"That was a close one," said the inflated-hand boy. "I'm Billy, by the way."

"Murph," said Murph, holding out his hand.

"Yeah, I know who you are. Kid Nor—"

"Don't even go there, Balloon Boy," said Murph, but with a smile.

"Heeey," said Billy. "If you get to call me Balloon Boy, then you're Kid Normal."

"Billy it is, then," Murph decided.

"Nice to meet you, Murph," replied Billy. "I quite like Balloon Boy, as a matter of fact. Anyway, have a seat. I've got some garlic bread left."

14

Captain Brush

As January went on, Billy spent more and more time with Mary, Hilda, and Murph. "We're like a crime-fighting team!" enthused Hilda once, but she fell silent as the other three looked at her with eyes that asked, "Seriously?"

But no sooner had Murph's life at school started to seem like something he might be able to cope with than, out of nowhere, the rug was not only pulled from beneath his feet but yanked, thrown into the corner, and set on fire. And guess who was standing there holding the matches? Correct. Once again it was the bristling, shouty Mr. Flash bearing the bad news.

A couple of weeks after the Great Tomato Sauce Incident, Murph and Billy had wandered to the library to avoid going outside into the raw January weather. It was a large, comfortable room with a calm atmosphere that was only rarely interrupted by a gentle **boop** as the librarian, Mrs. Fletcher, checked out books with her computer.

I wonder what her Cape is, Murph found himself thinking as they settled into two comfy chairs near the window. Idly he imagined Mrs. Fletcher firing flames out of her hands, or leaping tall buildings with her pleated, plum-colored skirt flapping in the breeze. It crossed his mind that her glasses, which were fastened around her neck on a delicate metal chain, could actually be very useful in a rescue situation. *You'd never lose them*, he thought. *And you could also use the loop as a lasso to reel in the bad guy.* Murph's imagination, as ever, was getting the better of him. Ironically, he was only minutes away from finding out what Mrs. Fletcher's Capability actually was, when Mr. Flash barged into the library like a wrecking ball.

"COOPER!" he barked, looking around like an angry lighthouse.

Mrs. Fletcher bristled. **"Shhhhhhh,"** she hissed sharply.

Mr. Flash tried again. **"COOPER!"** he husked, in one of the loudest whispers ever recorded.

"Oh nooooo," whined Billy, sliding down behind his chair, "he's gonna shout at us. He's still angry about getting covered in saaaaaauce." But it wasn't sauce that Mr. Flash had come to discuss. He spotted Murph in his seat beside the window and strode over, his huge boots clonking on the floor. Mrs. Fletcher went bright pink and made another angry shushing noise.

"Cooper," began Mr. Flash in an even more strangled voice. "I have some news for you. Now that I've got to start preparing the class for their P-CAT, obviously there's not much point you being in my lessons."

Oh great! thought Murph. *This is where he tells me I can hang out in the library for an hour every morning.*

"But you're not going to be hanging around in the library every morning," roared Mr. Flash unhelpfully. Behind him, Mrs. Fletcher got up from her librarian's chair, looking furious and shushing like a nearly boiled kettle. "You're going to be helping out Carl while the rest of us have CT." Mr. Flash looked like he was enjoying himself enormously.

"The janitor?" asked Murph blankly.

"That's right. You'll be the right-hand man's right-hand man," Mr. Flash went on. "So in the morning, you head to Carl's and see what you can help out with, and leave the rest of us to get on with some work. **_ALL RIGHT?_**"

Mr. Flash had gradually become aware that someone was standing right beside him, breathing heavily. Nervously, he turned his head and found himself staring into the furious eyes of Mrs. Fletcher.

"This is a library," she began angrily, "and I . . . said . . . **shush.** So would you please . . . **shush.**"

"All right, Mrs. Mouse, just giving Cooper here some good news. Keep your pants on."

"I beg your pardon . . . ," began Mrs. Fletcher.

"You heard. Don't get your hair in a twist. It's too quiet in here anyway."

At this point Mrs. Fletcher lost her temper. And this is where Murph found out what her Capability was. Because when Mrs. Fletcher boils over, her head transforms into a very large foghorn. And you know what noise a very large foghorn makes.

"PAAAAAAAAARP!"

went Mrs. Fletcher's foghorn head,
directly into Mr. Flash's face.

And then again. Twice more.

"PAAAAAAAARP!
PAAAAAAARP!"

After the three blasts, the entire library was silent from shock and awe.

Mr. Flash looked rather dazed and rather windswept. He reached up and wiped some librarian spit off his face, adjusted his mustache, and quietly walked off.

Mrs. Fletcher's head transformed back into a normal-size librarian head and she sat down as if nothing had happened.

The following morning, instead of heading to CT, Murph trudged off to begin his glamorous role as janitor's assistant. After Mr. Flash had left the library, Billy had informed Murph that Carl had a workshop on the edge of the woods at the back of The School grounds.

As Murph crossed the soccer fields, he realized

for the first time how large and cleverly laid out the grounds of The School were. The green fields behind the main buildings were almost totally secluded, with high wooden fences stretching into the distance and only a few treetops visible beyond. The School was on the edge of a steep ridge, he figured out, and because the ground dropped away so sharply, the whole place was practically invisible.

Perched on the edge of a slope near the trees was a collection of wooden buildings that, as Murph approached, he saw was bigger than it looked from a distance.

Carl's workshops tumbled down the first part of the slope on a cleverly stepped series of platforms. It was as if a building had been pushed off the edge of the hill and come to rest mid-collapse. There were extremely large double doors to the left—securely padlocked—that seemed to lead into a garage of some kind. To the right was a smaller door, which looked like the main entrance; there were large flowerpots on either side of it, although at this time of year they contained nothing but brown earth and the remains of the morning frost on top. And pinned up just beside the door was a small, grubby square of cardboard with the words *Fortress of Solitude* written in small, neat, curly handwriting. Next to them, in a different pen, someone else had drawn a smiley face.

Murph screwed his face up into the "other people are confusing" expression that he was now adopting for around 67 percent of the school day, and knocked on the door.

"Around the back," came a voice from the woods below him. Along the side of the building, Murph noticed a walkway of planks and paving stones that led crookedly down the hill and around to the back of the buildings. He picked his way down, heading toward a large pond he could make out through the trees. Overlooking the pond was a wide deck supported on stilts, and Murph caught a glimpse of a wisp of grayish smoke rising from it.

The smoke was emerging from a short wooden pipe stuck into the underside of a neat gray mustache. Above the mustache was a checked brown cap, and in between the two of them was a pair of shrewd eyes.

Two muddy leather boots finished off this whole arrangement, stretched out comfortably in front of an old-fashioned deck chair.

"Kid Normal," he said, drawing the words out speculatively and gazing at Murph through the cloud of smoke that came with them.

Murph realized that though he had seen the janitor zipping around The School plenty of times, he'd only once actually heard him speak before. His voice had a reassuring old-man huskiness to it, but it was deeper and more confident than he'd been expecting.

Murph half raised a hand in a nervous wave.

"Mr. Flash said I should come and help you out," he explained. "I'm off CT because I don't, you know . . ." He trailed off.

"Because you don't have a Cape," the janitor finished for him. "Because Geoffrey Souperman signed you up to The School thinking you were a skimmer, and now he's too embarrassed to admit he's made a massive mistake."

That about sums it up, thought Murph, signifying this by raising his eyebrows slightly and puffing out his cheeks.

"I'm Carl Walden. Pleased to meet you. Well, what *can* you do, then, Kid Normal? Can you hold a brush?"

Murph bristled. "Of course I can hold a brush. Holding a brush isn't a superpower—sorry, a Capability. Who would watch a film about the adventures of the amazing Captain Brush?"

"Who would watch a film about a perfectly ordinary kid?" countered Carl, which was unanswerable.

Murph did not answer, proving this to be true.

"Right then, Captain Brush," continued the janitor,

"time to put your amazing powers into action. The School is under threat! Only you can save the day. You'll find your secret weapon in the cupboard behind me." He jerked his head in the direction of a rough wooden door in the back wall of the outbuildings. "Sweep out the workshop for me. I'll be here if you need anything." He settled back in his chair as Murph went inside, leaving Carl to gaze out over the calm waters of the pond in the woods.

It was warm inside the workshop, and it carried the reassuring smell of sawdust, glue, and paint. A long wooden bench ran along the entire length of the room on one side, and above it was a board covered with every imaginable kind of tool, all neatly arranged in special clamps or hanging from hooks. There were intriguing contraptions everywhere: something motorcycle-shaped sat in one corner, covered by a cream-colored cloth, and weird-looking weapons lined another wall. One had a large iron grappling hook sticking out of the end.

Murph found a broom and began sweeping half-heartedly, all the while taking in this mysterious place.

On one shelf was a collection of angels, some made out of pottery, some wooden, with big faces, small faces, elaborate wings, and broken wings. A series of metal clamps, one of which Carl seemed to have been using recently, ran along the edge of the main workbench. There was a small pile of metal shavings on the floor underneath and a selection of tools strewn across the worktop nearby. Held in the clamp was a metal wristwatch.

Murph swept his way in that direction to get a better look. The watch had a lot of buttons, and he wondered what they could all possibly be for. Unable to resist the urge to find out, he touched one tentatively. Maybe it was one of those watches that could change the channel on the TV?

A jet of flame shot out of the side of the watch and singed a nearby potted plant.

Safe to say it isn't one of those TV-remote watches, thought Murph, dashing over and furiously trying to pat out the smouldering begonia.

"Everything all right in there, Captain Brush?" came Carl's voice from outside.

"Yep, absolutely! Just brooming away!" lied Murph, as a burning leaf drifted delicately to the floor.

As he was dusting the ash from the workbench, his attention was caught by something even more interesting than a flamethrower watch. Tucked away behind the plant was a wooden box full of photographs with its lid half off. Murph took a closer look and saw a face he recognized.

He carefully slid the photo out, trying not to disturb the stack or start any more fires.

It was a large black-and-white image of two men with their arms around each other and their thumbs up. One of the men was Mr. Souperman, dressed in the red costume Murph now knew belonged to his alter ego, Captain Alpha.

The other man, he realized with a thrill, was a much younger Carl—with no mustache, but still dressed in the same clothes and wearing his distinctive checked cap. Both men were smiling, standing in front of a car with a long hood, which was dented and scorched. But as Murph peered at it, trying to make out more details, he heard the door handle behind him turn.

In the nick of time he stuffed the photograph back into the stack, on top of a picture of a smiling girl with long silvery hair, and grabbed his broom just as Carl appeared in the doorway.

"Cup of tea, Captain?" the janitor asked.

Murph composed himself, but found his voice coming out higher than usual—the universal indicator of guilt. "Yes, please."

"Right you are," replied Carl. "Try not to start any more fires while I get the kettle on, eh? That's a good kid."

15

Heroes to Zeroes

At Ribbon Robotics, Nicholas Knox was sitting in an extremely comfortable office chair. It was upholstered in the finest leather and shone almost as brightly as his shoes, which were tucked neatly underneath him. Above the desk in front of him were three enormous computer screens, each of them displaying a patchwork of different video feeds. His gray-blue eyes flicked across them, scanning for likely prey.

Knox's drones, formally Penny Percival's drones—tiny robot wasps equipped with a camera—had been sent out far and wide, searching for people to control.

He had tried gyms, army camps, universities—but Knox was not satisfied. You see, he was an ambitious man—but he was ambitious for all the wrong things, as most ambitious people are. He was the sort of person who would demand the most expensive thing on the menu whether he liked it or not. If you plunked a can of cold beans in a bowl but charged two hundred dollars for it, that's what he'd want for lunch. So when it came to building his own private army of human servants—*Nektar's* private army, Knox reminded himself, at least for now—it had to be made up of the very best recruits. He was looking for something . . . special.

Knox reached forward with a long, mean-looking finger and tapped on one of the squares of video. It enlarged to focus on a military exercise going on in the hills on the outskirts of the town. Tough-looking soldiers were trekking up a slope with heavy backpacks, sweating despite the cold winter air.

Knox sighed. He'd been tracking this unit for a few days now—they were training to join the army's special elite forces and they seemed like the best. But somehow he still wasn't satisfied. If he brainwashed these soldiers and used them to try and seize power— if *Nektar* used them, he reminded himself again, at least for now—they'd just be met by other soldiers, many more of them. It wasn't going to be enough.

He leaned forward and spoke into a microphone on the desk: "Drone 445, disengage. Track alternative targets."

There was a small, pleasing **ping** and the soldiers on the video became smaller and smaller as the robot wasp abandoned its spying mission and flew onward, searching for something more interesting to film.

A few weeks on from his first day working alongside Carl, Murph had arrived at The School early as usual and taken up his customary position at the "early drop desk." It was a miserable day outside, rain hammering down—one of those days where you'd actually sprint into school just to get dry. As he sat there shivering, Flora appeared with a cup of tea and a chessboard. She'd taken to dropping in on Murph at his early-morning position, and had been teaching him chess in between chats about how he was managing at The School.

That morning, Flora was explaining what a "bare king" was as they waited for his friends to arrive. This usually happened in a very particular order.

Billy was always late, and he always had an excuse. To be fair to him, it was normally because he'd accidentally inflated a part of his body to such a degree that he couldn't get out of the house, let alone into his long-suffering mom's car. Mary was always prompt, though Murph now knew that the first day they'd met was one of the last times she'd traveled into school via her yellow umbrella. Soon afterward, Mr. Flash had caught her on the sports fields, preparing to fly home, and had shouted at her for a full ten minutes.

"ARE YOU TRYING TO GET YOURSELF CAUGHT, YOU RIDICULOUS YELLOW

CREATURE?" he'd bellowed, almost turning the umbrella inside out. **"DO YOU WANT TO BRING THE CLEANERS DOWN ON US? NO. FLYING. OUTSIDE. MY. CLASSROOM!"**

Mary had walked to and from school after that, except on very cloudy and wet days, when she was confident she wouldn't be seen by anyone, least of all Mr. Flash.

After Mary, Hilda would be next, dropped off in her father's old, green, but absolutely pristine Rolls Royce. It purred as it pulled up outside The School gates. It was the sort of car you'd imagine the queen to travel in, and Murph always found it odd that it was Hilda and not Her Majesty who jumped out, pigtails swinging, clasping a lunchbox—round-faced and rosy-cheeked Hilda, oblivious to everything around her. Even the rain. Just the very sight of her made Murph smile.

That day was no exception. Mary was first as usual, dashing in out of the rain and flumphing her umbrella just as Flora was finishing her chess tutorial: "And that's called a 'bad bishop.'"

"Right," said Murph. "Bare king, bad bishop. Better than a bad king, I guess."

"Or a bare bishop, for that matter," replied Flora. "Well, see you later."

Hilda came through the door at that moment, and she and Mary cornered Murph for an update on the mysterious photo he'd seen in Carl's workshop.

"Have you found out anything else about him? Do you think he used to be operational?" Hilda wanted to know. Despite Mr. Flash's contempt for her horses and Mr. Drench's refusal to say any more about his days as a Hero, she was still fascinated with the mysterious world of the Heroes' Alliance.

"I haven't managed to find out anything else yet," Murph said, "but I'm keeping my eyes open, don't worry. How's CT going, anyway? What's Flash been doing now he hasn't had a muffin to torch in weeks?"

"Well, it's all just P-CAT, P-CAT, P-CAT, nonstop," said Mary, "but he still won't tell us anything about it. He just says we'll need our wits about us."

"I know it's going to be awful," said Billy in a panicky voice. He'd just puffed his way damply through the doors and caught the end of the conversation. "I heard some of the older kids laughing about it. Hero Day, they call it. I'm no Hero! I bet it's some really scary tasks we have to do. It even *sounds* terrifying—P-CAT. Like a fierce alien robot cat. From space!" Billy was working himself up into a frenzy.

"Calm down," Hilda soothed him. "They're not going to give us anything we can't deal with."

Hilda, Mary, and Billy said goodbye to Murph and began heading off toward their CT lesson. Murph was just about to brave the weather and make his way down to Carl's sheds when something caught his attention outside the rainy front windows of The School.

A small figure darted across the schoolyard and disappeared into the coatroom, followed by five much larger figures.

"What's going on there?" Murph wondered out loud.

"What did you say?" called Mary, who had overheard him down the corridor.

"Oh, don't worry. Just something weird over in the coatrooms. I'll have a look on my way to Carl's," replied Murph.

Mary seemed eager to come back and see, but Billy tugged her away, terrified to be late for Mr. Flash.

Murph got up from his desk and headed across the front yard.

As he peeked into the coatroom, his heart sank. He recognized them instantly: it was the goons from his lunchroom plate-smashing incident. There they all were: Gangly Fuzz Face, Pork Belly Pig Breath, Corned Beef Boy, Crazy Eyes Jemima, and Frankenstein's Nephew. He still didn't know their real names.

Then, with a sinking heart, Murph spotted the smaller figure they had followed into the coatroom. It was Nellie, the girl with green ends to her hair who could control storm clouds. Murph was worried she wouldn't be able to get herself out of this one. She wasn't the greatest talker; in fact, Murph couldn't remember a time she'd *ever* spoken, so she certainly wasn't going to start outwitting this gang of lumps now—who, incidentally, were now surrounding her at the back of the otherwise empty coatroom.

"Come on, then," grunted Pork Belly Pig Breath, "make the rain disappear if you can—we want to go down to the shop and spend all your money."

Frankenstein's Nephew laughed. Nellie tried to push between two of them and run out of the coatroom, but stopped abruptly as if she'd run into an invisible force field.

She had. Gangly Fuzz Face had used one of his force fields on her.

"Oh, I don't think so," sneered

Gangly Fuzz Face as he used his Cape to drag Nellie back until she was pinned against the wall. "Come on, weather girl. If you can't stop the rain, we'll settle for your lunch money."

Nellie was glaring at them as if she was about to say something really rude but couldn't quite make the words get past her lips. Murph wanted to help, but didn't know how. The five of them would crush him into a jam, put him in an attractive jar, and sell him at the annual Christmas Craft Fair. And Murph hated Christmas Craft Fairs. He hated the fact that he couldn't pluck up the courage to do something. He was so frustrated with himself that he made a small growling noise.

"Who's there?" barked Gangly Fuzz Face.

Before Murph knew it, a meaty hand had plucked him out of the coats like a claw picks up teddy bears in one of those carnival machines. Unfortunately, unlike the claws at carnivals, the hand didn't drop him.

Instead he was plunked down beside Nellie by Corned Beef Boy. He looked even more meat-like up close.

Murph realized there was no avoiding it: he was going to have to stand up for himself and Nellie. It was five against two. And the five were as big as the two were small. He thought he'd lead off with that fact.

"Oh yeah, really heroic, guys—five of you picking on two of the new students," said Murph.

"What are you talking about?" snarled Crazy Eyes Jemima. "We've got four of you now."

"No, we haven't," sighed Gangly Fuzz Face quietly. "Why don't you ever remember your glasses?"

"Great," said Murph. "One of you can count at least."

"Easy now, little buddy. Don't get cocky with us. Remember what happened the last time," said Gangly Fuzz Face. "And as we've just established, there are only two of you."

"Make that five!" said a voice behind him.

Mary, Billy, and Hilda were silhouetted in the doorway.

"You guys are pathetic!" jeered Mary to the assorted freak show. "You really think the Alliance is going to be impressed? 'Oh, great, I'm in trouble. I know what I'll do. I'll call for those bullying idiots that think stealing people's money is okay.'"

It's a good thing there was no sarcasm detector nearby. It probably would have exploded.

"Well, look who we've got here. A little yellow birdy," sneered Gangly Fuzz Face, taking in Mary's yellow dress and umbrella. "What's your name—Mary Canary?"

"Well, normally they just call me Mary," said Mary confidently.

"Do you live in a dairy?" guffawed Corned Beef Boy.

"Er, yes, how did you know that?" asked Mary, momentarily confused. But she rallied admirably. "Anyway, we're not talking about me. We're talking about you abusing your Capes by bullying new students and trying to steal from them. Can't wait to let Mr. Flash know what sort of Heroes he's training in your grade."

Amazingly, Mary's words seemed to have hit home. The bullies shuffled about awkwardly. Mary didn't know, but they were actually some of Mr. Flash's favorite students and he had them tagged for great things. They were indeed hoping he'd recommend them to the Heroes' Alliance.

"We were only joking. We weren't really going to take her money," mumbled Gangly Fuzz Face.

"Well, let me tell you, that is a stupid joke," replied Hilda tartly. "Come on, Murph, come on, Nellie, let's leave these creeps hanging around the junior coatroom."

Murph sailed past Frankenstein's Nephew and Corned Beef Boy like a tiny tugboat between two ugly old battleships. Nellie trailed after him with her hair hanging over her face and one damp untied shoelace flapping behind her.

All five of them walked out of the coatroom unscathed.

"We did it!" enthused Hilda in a whisper. "We stuck together and defeated the forces of evil! We're Heroes!" And there was definitely a spring in their step as they marched away from the coatroom. Mary, in high spirits, put up her yellow umbrella and used it to leap over a large puddle.

"Can you even fly without that stupid umbrella, Mary Canary?" came a cruel voice from behind them.

Gangly Fuzz Face and his cohorts had gathered in the coatroom doorway to get the last word. "You think we're never going to make it as Heroes? What about you losers? A kid with no Cape and his dumb friends? Heroes? ZEROES more like! HA HA! There they go, look. The SUPER ZEROES!"

The rest of his herd started laughing too.

"Yeah, Super Zeroes! Good one!" chortled Crazy Eyes Jemima. "You'd better stay out of our way, Super Zeroes . . . all ten of you!"

16

Expectations

It was February, and Murph's hands were nearly frozen to the broom as Carl sent him to sweep the front porch of the wooden shed that stood at one side of the soccer fields.

The shed was used by Mr. Flash to store the accessories he used for outdoor CT lessons: special catapults that fired large clay discs into the air for target practice, huge sheets of corrugated iron, piles of old traffic cones, and the like. The porch itself was scorched and gouged with what looked like huge claw marks.

As Murph moodily flicked piles of frozen dead leaves out onto the grass, his heart sank. His whole class was heading across the field toward him, led by Mr. Flash himself. Despite the cold weather, he was wearing his normal uniform of army fatigues and a tight black sleeveless shirt. His muscled arms were bare, and his breath steamed underneath his red mustache in the frosty morning air, making him look a bit like a cigar-smoking walrus.

"WOW, ALL THE SUPER ZEROES TOGETHER, WOULD YOU LOOK AT THAT!" yelled Mr. Flash delightedly as he approached. Gangly Fuzz Face and his friends had wasted no time in telling as many people as possible about their nickname for the kid with no Cape and his friends, and Mr. Flash, predictably, had found it hilarious. Murph caught Mary's eye, and she made a lemon-sucking face. "Normal, grab us a bucket of nails, will you? Make yourself useful." A couple of Flash's favorites giggled.

Murph dropped his broom and trudged into the shed. He grabbed a bucket filled with metal nails and marched back outside, where Mr. Flash was waiting with his hand held out.

"Excellent fetching capability, Normal," he leered, "positively doglike."

More giggling. Murph gritted his teeth.

"So," continued the teacher, "let's see how Natalie's coming on, shall we? You get on with the sweeping, kid," he added as an aside to Murph. "This doesn't concern you."

Turning back to the rest of the class, Flash roared, "**RIGHT!** Natalie tells me she would like to attempt to develop her Cape to an operational standard. Great to have ambition. Always aim to have ambition, that's what I say. As long as you know that you have an almost completely nonexistent chance of achieving that ambition. **ALL RIGHT?**" He shouted the last word so loudly that he startled a cow fully half a mile away.

"In fact," continued Mr. Flash, "let me manage your expectations. Imagine this muffin represents your expectations of becoming a Hero."

He turned to Murph and held a hand out, clicking his fingers.

You have got to be kidding me, thought Murph, pulling his break-time muffin out of his large coat pocket, where he'd been keeping it safe like a baby hedgehog, and reluctantly handing it over.

Mr. Flash threw the muffin high into the air. The class squinted into the bright winter sky as it reached the top of its trajectory and started to fall back to earth.

"So, the muffin is your expectations, right?" clarified Mr. Flash, adopting a kung-fu stance with his left leg in the air. The muffin was almost at head height.

Then he moved so fast that there seemed to be at least eight separate muscly, mustachioed men chopping at the muffin with their hands. That's not a sentence you read every day, and here comes another one.

The air was so thick with crumbs that it was like a scene from the horror film that cakes would make if they had video cameras and thumbs.

"Expectations managed?" asked Mr. Flash, licking a stray crumb from the eastern branch of his mustache. "Even if you pass the P-CAT and you're in my classes from next year, your chance of becoming an operational Hero—of joining the Alliance—is still practically zero."

Mr. Flash was not what you'd call an inspirational teacher.

"Where was I?" he went on in more measured tones. "Ah yes, Natalie's been developing her Cape—which is technically known as magnetic manipulation." He picked up the bucket of nails, irritably swatting away a wasp that was buzzing around his head.

Natalie, a neatly dressed girl with dark hair cut in a bob, marched confidently to the front of the class and took up her position in the middle of the scattering of muffin crumbs.

"Right, see how many you can get," shouted Mr. Flash, flinging the bucket forward and upward so that the nails flew into the air. Natalie screwed up her face in concentration. Murph watched in amazement as the nails stopped in their trajectory, as if a huge magnet was pulling them toward Natalie. Some of the nails closest to her flew to the palms of her outstretched hands and stuck there sideways. Others fell to the ground.

"Now concentrate," said Mr. Flash. "See if you can get a few more."

Natalie's forehead was beaded with sweat. Her eyes bulged as she strained as hard as she could. Murph could see a nail on the ground not far from him begin to quiver.

Suddenly Natalie screamed. The wasp that had been annoying Mr. Flash had flown to her hand and stuck to it, buzzing angrily.

A wasp in the hand, as you may know, is worth really freaking out over—and Natalie was really freaking out. She shook her hand frantically, trying to dislodge the wasp and sending nails flying in all directions, like the world's most twisted piñata. Mr. Flash's form blurred as he rushed to her side, grabbed the wasp, and crushed it under the sole of his heavy black boot.

As the class clustered around, Murph turned back to his broom, wondering two things: What was a wasp doing flying about in February? And, more importantly, why had it been attracted to Natalie's hand?

Was it possible, he thought, *to have a wasp . . . made of metal?*

On the other side of town, Nicholas Knox bent excitedly toward his central computer screen. He reached out a long finger, swiping backward and forward through the footage from his camera drone.

He watched the large man darting back and forth with superhuman speed as he chopped and kicked at what appeared to be a bakery product of some kind. He watched the girl with dark hair who could apparently attract metal to her hands like a magnet. He looked at the other children in the class.

They didn't seem at all surprised by any of it, thought Knox. *Was it possible they had these kinds of powers as well?*

He leaned back in his chair and laced his hands behind his head, plotting like nobody's business. *A school*, he mused. *A very special school. A school . . . for superheroes?* He would have to tell Nektar about this intriguing discovery. But not quite yet. First he needed to know more.

Knox spoke into his microphone: "All drones, repeat, all drones, abandon assignments. Report to last-known coordinates of drone 445 for further reconnaissance. Activate."

The small **ping** noise sounded, and across his three screens the video feeds blurred as his robot wasps turned away from whatever else they had been spying on and headed for the sky, ready to seek out their new target.

Murph had scooped up the crushed bits of wasp and decided to show them to Carl. It was now bitingly cold and had started to hail. He bundled himself up as best he could and headed back across the soccer fields, leaning into the wind like an Antarctic hero. He could only just make out Carl's ramshackle collection of sheds through the driving white lumps that stung his eyes and face. But there was a thin stream of smoke coming out of the tin chimney on top of the right-hand shed, and that hope of warmth was enough to keep him going until, a few breathless minutes later, he was knocking on Carl's wooden door with a numb red hand.

The rasping noise he could hear from inside stopped. There were footsteps, and then Carl tugged the door open. Murph gratefully slipped through it.

"Morning, Captain Brush. Lovely day for it," Carl greeted him drily, and returned to filing a long piece of metal clamped to his workbench.

"Carl, can a wasp be made of metal?" asked Murph hesitantly. Carl stopped work and turned to look at him expectantly. "Because I was just watching a CT lesson out there, and a girl with magnetic powers attracted a wasp to her hand."

"Hard to tell without a sample," said Carl, raising his eyebrows under his flat cap.

Murph opened his hand, revealing a few pieces of smashed wasp coated in mud. Carl took them, and together they walked to the back of the building, where a large magnifying glass was set up on a flexible stand underneath a lamp. Carl poured the wasp parts onto the table underneath the glass and peered through the lens intently.

"Interesting," he muttered. "Haven't seen anything like that before. And this thing was just buzzing around the CT lesson, was it?"

Murph nodded.

Carl looked grim, the wrinkles around his eyes creasing together. "Looks like someone's taking an interest in us. And we're not too keen on that here. Nice work, Normal. I'll keep an eye on this, and you keep an eye out as well."

Murph had a sudden thought: "Do you think this is connected to the wasp story in the papers? It's got to be!" he decided.

"Sounds likely, doesn't it?" answered Carl. "Now clear off back into the blizzard and get yourself to your next class before you're late. I've got some work to do in there."

He indicated a door to the side of the workshop— which Murph guessed must lead to the large area behind the garage doors at the front of the building.

It was securely padlocked and had a sign saying **"No admittance under any circumstances"** on it.

"What's in there?" Murph wanted to know, along with the rest of us.

Carl, one hand on his bunch of keys, ready to open the door, turned back to him and may or may not have winked.

"Secrets," he said unhelpfully. "Now scram."

Unfortunately, Murph's warning had come too late. Because over the next few hours, more and more of Nektar's spy drones converged on The School. The next day one managed to get through the window into the CT lesson and witnessed Elsa making delicate icicles appear from the ceiling as she honed her Capability with the help of Mr. Drench. Another spied on Mr. Souperman as he casually lifted his entire desk up with one hand to retrieve a dropped pen. And it was all beamed back across town to Ribbon Robotics, where Nicholas Knox stamped his shiny shoes in delight. This school could provide him with an army that would be unbeatable. With servants like this, he could do anything he wanted.

"This school could provide you with an army that would be unbeatable," Knox told Nektar later that day. "With servants like this, you could do anything you wanted."

Nektar's bulbous insect eyes flashed greedily as he sucked on a plastic jug of maple syrup like a weird giant wasp baby.

"And you're sure we can mount a successful picnic?" he asked.

"Picnic?" queried Knox.

"Attack, I said, attack. Mount a successful attack. Stop mentioning picnics!" buzzed Nektar peevishly.

"Apologies, sir." Nicholas Knox bowed insincerely. "With time to plan, yes, I'm confident. With your permission I shall continue to monitor this school and give you regular reports."

But Nektar had lost interest already, as Gary had come into the room with a fresh tray of lemonade and a large tub of ice cream.

Knox didn't stay to find out what weirdness was about to ensue. He swept from the room and returned to his lair to continue spying.

 Over the following weeks, Knox learned much more

about The School. His tiny robot wasps positioned themselves invisibly in classrooms, hallways, and the auditorium. On his screens Knox's greedy eyes read the Heroes' Vow. He listened in to lessons and eavesdropped on teachers in the staffroom.

But as winter began to thaw into spring, he overheard one particular conversation that gave him his greatest and most daring idea . . .

Flora popped her head into Mr. Souperman's office: "Iain Flash is here to see you, Geoffrey."

The headmaster was standing at the window with his hands on his hips, idly watching a wasp that was crawling down the glass. "Ah yes, thank you," he said.

Mr. Flash stomped in, rudely shoving past Flora, who stuck her tongue out at him behind his back before disappearing off to her desk.

"You wanted to see me, headmaster?" barked Mr. Flash, sounding as if he had somewhere more important to be, which of course he didn't.

"Yes, Iain, I just wanted to check that everything's in place for your P-CAT next week?" asked the headmaster.

"Anything you need? It's the most important day of the school year, after all, and I don't want anything to go wrong."

"All in hand, all in hand, don't worry," Mr. Flash assured him aggressively. "It's not my first time, you know. Not that I hold out much hope that any of this lot will be able to make it past many of the obstacles."

"Well, not a lot of them usually do, as far as I remember," mused Mr. Souperman. "Please try not to injure too many of them this year, though. The whole school will be watching."

"But that's what it's all about, isn't it?" challenged Flash. "A chance to showcase the best of the best. See how they perform against my assault course and two actual working Alliance operatives."

"Ah yes, so the Posse will act as your assistants this year?"

"Yep. They'll be my eyes and ears. And hands, in fact."

"Yes, well—" began Mr. Souperman.

"And legs," added Mr. Flash. "Because they'll be running about—"

"Yes, I understand, thank you," the headmaster cut

in. "And while you're here, how is young Mr. Cooper getting along?"

"Kid Normal?" scoffed Mr. Flash. "Who knows? He's off in the shed with Carl every morning now, rather than holding back my CT class. Best place for him. I still don't know what you were thinking, letting someone without a Cape remain here."

Mr. Souperman glanced toward the door.

"Yes, with that in mind, perhaps we should keep him out of the way during the P-CAT. I don't think a boy without a Cape is likely to have much to offer—he might just be a distraction for the other students. Find him something to do during the day to keep him busy, will you?" instructed Mr. Souperman.

"Will do, sir!" replied Mr. Flash happily.

Listening in on his screens on the other side of town, Nicholas Knox realized he had discovered the ideal moment for his attack. It couldn't be more perfect. The whole school would be together; there would be two actual working *superheroes* there—he still couldn't quite believe it. Knox itched to know more about their powers, and waited hungrily for the chance to question his captives. He knew he'd never get a better opportunity to capture himself an army in one fell swoop.

"You'll never get a better opportunity to capture yourself an army in one fell swoop, sir," he informed Nektar soon afterward. "With my spies guiding you in, you can use the new attack drones to take over The School. If you mind-control the most powerful people first, they can then assist you, and the rest of the operation should present no problems."

"Me? You're not coming with me?" Nektar looked worried.

"I need to coordinate the operation from here, sir. But don't worry, we'll be in constant contact. And remember, you'll be protected by the attack drones at all times. There is no possible danger," finished Knox, sounding as sincere as possible.

And so they began to plan their attack.

Murph had really started to enjoy his time helping Carl. Since he'd brought the metal wasp to his attention, the janitor seemed to trust him more. Carl had spent hours examining the crushed fragments, but had been unable to figure out much more about the mysterious machine from the tiny fragments Mr. Flash's boot-pulping had left behind. He had taken to patrolling The School with a makeshift magnetic swatter he'd cobbled together in his workshop, desperate to catch another wasp. He was unaware, though, that Knox's technology was far too advanced to let that happen. The tiny drones were too cunning and communicated with one another too effectively to let themselves be tracked down.

Carl had also informed Mr. Souperman, who had promised to pass the information on to what he called the "relevant authorities". But as the headmaster hadn't been listening to Carl properly at the time, he came away with a vague notion that the janitor had been complaining about an actual wasp. In fact, he forgot the conversation almost as soon as it had happened.

Carl occasionally discussed the metal wasp with Murph over steaming cups of tea as the wind howled outside the wooden workshop. But without any real information, they had no hope of working out what was actually going on. For Murph the chats also provided a chance to try and wheedle more details out of Carl about his past. He noticed that the box of photographs had disappeared from its place on the bench, and Carl was much too sharp to let any details slip.

Still, they both enjoyed each other's company, and Carl even let Murph help out with a few of the gadgets he spent his days putting together. As a treat, Murph was actually allowed to take home the odd prototype here and there, as long as he promised no one would see it.

One Tuesday, Murph ran home, ready to dart up to his room as quickly as possible to play with something Carl called a Grapple Gun, a small pistol that fired a length of strong rope that could be used for climbing or grabbing things a long way away.

But as he reached the house, he realized something was wrong. His brother had shut himself in his room and his mom was sitting at the table in their tiny dining room with her head in her hands.

As soon as Murph saw her he knew what had happened. He'd been here three times before. Quickly stuffing the Grapple Gun into a rain boot standing just inside the front door, he steeled himself for the bad news.

"They're not keeping you on at work, are they?" he said bluntly.

Silently his mom shook her head, then seemed to decide she'd have to say something.

"Murph, I'm so sorry," she said unsteadily. "I realize you like it here—you've been much more like your old self these last few weeks. And believe me, I've done everything I can. And I'll keep trying, I promise."

"And what good's that going to do?" Murph suddenly felt furious. "This has happened four times now, Mom. Am I ever going to get to stay at a school for more than a year? Or is this it, now? Should I just give up on ever making any friends?"

"Well, I didn't know you even *had* any friends," his mom hit back at him. "You refuse to tell me anything much about this school. I mean, I was relieved to find you a place and it certainly seems to have cheered you up a bit. But what's the big secret, for goodness' sake?"

"Oh, what does it matter anyway?" replied Murph bitterly, turning away. "I'd better get ready to leave it all behind again, hadn't I?" And with that, he sulked out of the door and wandered around to stand on the bridge over the filthy canal.

The full realization of how upset he was about this began to sink in. For the first time in ages he'd started to make friends. But soon he'd have to say goodbye to Mary; to Billy, Hilda, and Nellie; Carl and his workshop; Flora; even Gangly Fuzz Face and his goons: all erased from his life. And he was sure that wherever his family ended up living after this, the next school wouldn't be half as interesting.

17

Soup

The day of Nektar's attack was unseasonably warm and clammy. Thick gray clouds hung over the town like a damp, dirty duvet. A faint rumble of thunder sounded in the distance, although it might just have been a dog's stomach making a noise not that far away. Frankly, it was too stuffy to care.

At Ribbon Robotics, Nektar was making his final preparations. He had emerged from his nest in a good mood that morning, looking forward to beginning the creation of his own private army. For this would bring him a step closer to taking control of the country, which would enable him to ban picnics, get stuck in ice cream, and buzz around trash cans to his stripy heart's content. He had breakfasted lightly on three chocolate bars and an entire gallon of orange juice that he'd slurped straight from the bottle with his long hollow tongue. Gary the intern had tried to point out the words "dilute to taste" on the label, but he'd been wasting his time.

Nicholas Knox was fussing over him like an overprotective mom on the first day at school. "Now, are you sure you've got everything, evil Lord Nektar?"

"Yes, Knox, I've got everything," snapped Nektar. He was dressed in his full yellow-and-black costume, with black boots, a yellow-and-black jumpsuit, and a helmet covering his bulging insect eyes. So rather than looking like an evil man-wasp hybrid, he looked like he was part of an insect-themed motorcycle stunt team. This was the first time since becoming an evil man-wasp that he was going to venture outside his factory, and he wanted to be prepared.

"Have you got the master uplink system for the mind-control helmets?" asked Knox.

"Of course I have," Nektar raged, his good mood ebbing away. "What would be the point of my going outside this factory for the first time to initiate my evil plan to take over the country using an army of human drones wearing mind-control helmets if I didn't take the master uplink system for the mind-control helmets with me?"

"Of course, sir," Knox reassured him. "It's just that the master uplink system for the mind-control helmets is over there on that table."

Nektar marched over and snatched up what looked like a big black watch, snapping it onto his wrist.

The master uplink system was the key to the whole mind-control technology Knox had invented. Whoever wore that black wristband would be able to command anyone wearing one of the helmets to do absolutely anything. It made you the master of an army of servants. Or, if you put the helmets on llamas, an army of llamas. A llama army. You could also dress them in nightgowns and force them to work in a field, making you the master of a pajama'd llama farmer army, but that might be taking things too far.

Nicholas Knox's fellow robotics expert, Penny Percival, was standing to one side. If you remember, she had once invented a fabulous rainbow robot fish that could have solved all the world's clean water problems until Nektar stamped on it. But in the last few months she had been working hard on a very different project. She had worked hard on it because Knox had snuck up behind her with a mind-control helmet and turned her into a helpless servant.

Penny's black-and-yellow eyes watched expressionlessly as Nektar turned to her and asked, "Human drone Percival, do you have the attack drones ready?"

"All is ready, mighty Lord Nektar," she replied in a monotone, and handed him a small remote-control unit. "Press the homing button in the center to summon the attack drones. They will respond to your commands, O powerful one."

Nektar grinned to himself. Being the commander of a drone army was super convenient. Though he was a little worried about Knox, who seemed to be getting rather too big for his extremely shiny shoes recently.

Never mind, thought Nektar inside his mean, waspy brain. *When I have my army of servants, I won't need him anymore.* He caught Knox's eye and smiled unconvincingly.

Knox gave a watery smile back, thinking to himself: *When I have my army of servants, I won't need him anymore.*

That's one of the main problems with being a

supervillain. It's really hard to get staff who don't end up plotting against you.

Nektar pressed the single yellow button on the black remote control and immediately there was a loud buzzing from the hallway outside. Gary ran past, making a terrified squeaking noise as Penny Percival's new inventions rounded the corner and came floating in through the open door. There were four of them: huge robot wasps the size of motorcycles.

They flew with the aid of rotor blades suspended from their metal backs. They had a black-muzzled machine gun fixed to each of their yellow-and-black-striped sides. And inside the gaping mouth of

each attack drone was a small blue flame—the pilot light for their built-in flamethrower.

Basically, since becoming a human drone, Penny had lowered her sights considerably from wanting to save the planet.

These machines had been built with one purpose: to destroy the enemies of whoever held the central control unit. Right now that person was Nektar, and he regarded them with delight.

He pressed the yellow button again. "Attack drones, maintain formation and protect me with full firepower," he commanded. The drones maneuvered themselves into position, two behind each of his yellow leather-clad shoulders.

Right, go and do my dirty work for me and bring me back a load of super-powered servants before I snatch the control units away from you and take control of this whole operation, said Nicholas Knox, but only to himself.

Out loud he said, "Your attack vehicles are ready in the front courtyard, mighty Nektar. The coordinates of The School have been preprogrammed. I shall monitor things from here using my spy drones and assist if necessary." He smiled awkwardly.

Nektar grimaced back at him before marching out of the room and into the elevator, humming a dramatic tune in his waspy voice. He was on course to take over the world. Nothing could stand in his way.

The elevator was out of order, and he had to go down the stairs.

The day of Nektar's attack was also the day that Murph decided there was absolutely no point to anything, least of all going to school. It was the morning after he'd discovered the news about his mom's job, and they had hardly spoken since. She had dropped him off early as usual, and he was now sitting moodily behind his empty desk in the entrance hall, doing some really hard-core scowling.

"Why are you even bothering going to work?" he'd grumped at her before she'd driven away. "They're getting rid of you. What's the point? And what's the point of sending me to school if we've got to move again in the summer?"

"The point is not to give up," his mom had snapped back at him. "We can't all roll into a ball and refuse to come out of the house just because we've got to move again, Murph." She softened as she saw how upset he was. "I hate it just as much as you do. Next year I promise I'll look for something that'll last for longer."

"You—"

"Said that last year," finished his mom. "I know." She sighed, but before she could think of any more mom wisdom, Murph had slammed the car door and trudged away across the road toward the empty school buildings.

And now here he was, looking forward to a morning of helping out Carl while the rest of his class honed their superhuman abilities. It was going to be a bad day.

Murph was working himself up into such a mood, he even began to feel bitter about his friends. They'd all have forgotten about him in a few weeks' time, he mused to himself furiously, just like last year, and the year before that. And when the next school year came around they'd just go on without him, while he tried to settle into another new town and another new school.

Murph had sunk into such a miserable state that he only grunted when Hilda walked past on her way to the coatroom, waving at him. He pretended not to hear Billy's shouted greeting. Mary came up and stamped her foot at him after he responded to her cheery "Morning, Murph!" with a growly **bleeurgh** noise.

"What's gotten into you today?" she demanded, but eventually walked off in a sulk when he refused to reply.

"I thought you'd say 'good luck' at least," she shouted over her shoulder at him. "We've got the P-CAT today."

Murph had actually forgotten that the rest of his class would be taking the P-CAT that day, the test that would determine which CT class they'd be in next year. He felt a tiny spark of pleasure pierce the gloom curtain: watching the test might be kind of fun. But once again, Mr. Flash appeared on the scene to smoosh his muffin of hope into crumbs of sadness.

"NORMAL!" he bellowed, striding toward him. "Welcome to Hero Day. Not that it concerns you. You won't be watching the P-CAT with the rest of The School," he continued, as if he were a mean-spirited mind reader. "Mr. Souperman's decided it would be best if you stay out of the way, so I've left a couple of buckets and a scrubbing brush in my classroom. Give the floor and the walls a good cleanup, would you? Some of the older

students got a little bit carried away with their Capes in Mr. Drench's lesson yesterday, particularly Gareth. He can summon soup whenever he likes, but he hasn't quite got it under control yet. Anyway, if you could clear up the minestrone, that'd be perfect."

And he marched off, muttering something about useless Capes and soup.

"Fine," said Murph to Mr. Flash's retreating back. "Great."

He grabbed his bag and was about to head toward the classroom. But suddenly, the whole thing seemed like an intolerable waste of time. Despite what his mom had said, going home and curling up in a ball was the only thing he felt like doing right now. He wasn't even going to be allowed to watch everyone take their P-CAT. It was the final insult. Murph looked around at the drab walls of the school hallway and felt he couldn't bear to spend another minute there.

Angrily, he shouldered his bag, and instead of moving toward the CT classroom to begin de-souping, he found himself walking right out of the doors and heading back across toward the school gates.

"Murph?" came a shout from behind him. It was Mary. **"Where are you going?"**

"I'm going home. I've had enough of this stupid school," yelled Murph, rounding on her. "You're all right; you've got a Cape. How do you think I feel? I'm only good enough to clean up soup! I don't even like soup."

"Why are you talking about soup?" asked Mary, who'd come back to make peace with Murph before her exam, and wasn't expecting to have an argument about soup. "And my Cape's nothing much to get excited about anyway—you know Mr. Flash thinks I'm useless because I can't do it without the umbrella! It's not just you."

"Oh, so I'm useless now?" snapped Murph.

"Of course you're not useless. I said Mr. Flash THINKS we're useless. But that's the point, isn't it? It doesn't matter what he thinks of you. He's a bully." Mary had planted her hands on her hips as she entered Lecture Mode. "And you know the thing about bullies, Murph? They're only powerful if you listen to them. Don't let him get to you!"

A part of Murph's brain tried to shake off the gloomy fog that was enveloping him, but it was stuck in place: an oily, suffocating cloud of depression. Even though her reasoning made sense—and actually reminded him of something his mom had said—it was too late. Mr. Flash *had* gotten to Murph. In fact, Murph's whole life had gotten to Murph, and for now he just needed to be on his own.

Ignoring Mary's disappointed face, he walked right through the school gates and headed for home.

He was so angry he didn't really register the four very large yellow-and-black trucks branded with the Ribbon Robotics logo that thundered past him in the other direction as he turned the corner at the end of the street. He didn't even hear the thin whining of the tiny spy wasp that followed him home.

18

Attack of the Killer Drones

Everyone at The School looked forward to Hero Day—the day of the P-CAT test—more than any other. Everyone except the youngest students, that is. For them, it was a terrifying jump into the unknown that no one would tell them much about.

For the rest, however, it was a chance to watch the younger kids take on an almost impossible assault course. It was a bit like watching a bunch of people jump into a freezing cold lake when you're already out, wrapped in a warm towel, and enjoying a hot chocolate.

Rows of bleachers had been set up on the soccer fields for the spectators, with wooden benches for the competitors. Boxes of ribbons and medals were being lugged up to the fields by some of Mr. Flash's least favorite students—he quite liked the irony of the least capable carrying awards for the most capable. But, then again, he would, wouldn't he? Not that many awards got handed out anyway—most years only three or four students got to the end of the P-CAT assault course.

A course that the youngest students were now regarding nervously.

It stretched the entire length of the sports fields, and it looked terrifying. Impossibly high climbing nets were slung from wooden posts, and beyond that there was a fence of vicious-looking barbed wire. Farther in the distance there was a tunnel to crawl through that seemed to be full of smoke. And right in front of their terrified eyes was a line of stout straw dummies with thick rope arms.

Deborah Lamington and Dirk Scott—aka the Posse— were also ready to take part. Deborah was positioned at the back of the soccer fields, not far from Carl's work- shops, beside a large pile of brightly colored plastic hula hoops. Dirk, holding two thick foam pads as tall as himself, was standing beside the pavilion expectantly.

"Right!" barked Mr. Flash, marching up and down in front of the nervous line of students. "This course has been expertly designed by me to test your abilities to the limit. Whether you're a skimmer, super-strong, or you've got a mental Cape like tele-tech, you should be able to figure out a way to get around most of these obstacles. Even if your Capability is"—he increased in volume slightly and glanced at Hilda—"utterly, completely useless, you may still be able to find a way through. Think about your Cape and try to fit it to the problem you're facing. But remember—this has been designed to simulate the conditions of a real mission. So just like in the real world, you're on your own. Don't expect anyone to back you up. And don't stop to help out the weaker ones. Only the very best will end up in my class next year and stand any chance of joining the Heroes' Alliance. Most of you don't have a hope in heck. Good luck!"

And with that, Mr. Flash darted over to Deborah at the other side of the field in a fraction of a second. The students could see him talking to her in the distance. Over on the bleachers, Mr. Souperman rose to his feet and addressed the whole school, holding a microphone to his mouth.

"Welcome, everyone, to the P-CAT test. We're all looking forward to seeing how many of our youngest students can complete the course this year." There was a chorus of jeers and shouts from the rest of the school—

clearly they didn't think many people would be getting to the finish line. Mr. Souperman calmed them with a wave of his right bicep: "Settle down, everyone. Right, Mr. Drench, are you ready?"

Mr. Drench was standing in the center of the course with a clipboard, apparently ready to assess the students' performance as they struggled with the obstacles. He waved a hand.

"Excellent," continued the headmaster. "Well, I think we can ask Mrs. Fletcher to sound the starting horn as soon as Mr. Flash is ready." The librarian was sitting at the corner of the stands, looking expectant.

Mr. Flash, who a second ago had been talking to Deborah, was suddenly back in front of the class again. He bent to whisper something to Dirk Scott, who lifted his foam pads and abruptly darted out of sight.

"READY?" screamed Mr. Flash at the class. Nobody said they were ready, but a second later he had made a chopping motion with his arm. This was Mrs. Fletcher's cue.

"PAAAAAAARP!" went the librarian's foghorn head.

"GO!" screamed Mr. Flash at lung-tearing volume. He started pushing the students one by one toward the line of straw dummies. They had now started spinning at incredible speed, their outstretched rope arms whistling as they cut through the air.

At the other side of the field, Deborah Lamington picked up her hula hoops and started skimming them across the course. They came fizzing along at around head height, forcing everyone to duck and weave as they ran toward the dummies.

Charlie, the boy who could burn muffins with his eyes, reached them first. For a moment it looked like he was going to use his Cape on the dummies and set one on fire, but almost immediately he got a thick rope arm in the face and fell over backward, stunned.

Everyone else hung back nervously, until Dirk Scott appeared behind them and started jabbing them all forward with his foam pads.

'THIS IS WHY NONE OF YOU ARE EVER GOING TO GET TAKEN ON BY THE ALLIANCE!'

screamed Mr. Flash. "Isn't anybody going to use their Cape, for Pete's sake? What's the matter with you all?"

Mary, Billy, Nellie, and Hilda were clustered together on one side of the course. Mary thought about flying over the obstacles, but every time she looked up, a bright plastic hoop skimmed above her head. One of Billy's hands inflated suddenly and he fell over sideways. Nellie kept her head down, hair covering her face.

"I wish Murph was here," muttered Hilda to herself. "He always makes me feel better."

The first of Nektar's four attack vehicles smashed through the school gates and skidded to a halt on the concrete area outside the main doors. Nektar climbed out of the passenger seat and surveyed the empty buildings, his huge attack wasps detaching themselves from the roofs of the trucks to hover beside him, bristling with firepower.

"Come in, Knox. It doesn't look like anyone's here."

The voice of Nicholas Knox crackled in his earpiece: "My spies indicate that the assault course is taking place on the grass area behind The School, Lord Nektar. All the students and teachers are assembled—it couldn't be more perfect for me—" He coughed and Nektar's earpiece crackled annoyingly. "For *you*," Knox corrected himself. "I do beg your pardon. If you use the drones to transport yourself over the school buildings, we should have the element of surprise. I can direct you to the best preliminary targets."

Back at the P-CAT assault course, Mr. Flash was still yelling at the class. "Use your Capabilities, you useless nitwits! Come on, think!"

But there wasn't much time to think with hula hoops flying around and dummies spinning in front of you. It was like a really weird dream, only one in which you actually got hit on the head. And a lot of the class were struggling to understand how this was supposed to relate to a real-life situation.

"Sir," asked Elsa breathlessly, after one of Deborah's missiles had knocked her to the ground, "do you come up against many flying hoops working as a crime-fighting superhero?"

"SHUT UP!" screamed Mr. Flash, turning so red he looked like a hairy-lipped lobster.

Suddenly there was a fizz and a spark from the electrical wire leading to the dummies, and they gradually stopped spinning. The class began to shove their way through.

"That's more like it," said Mr. Flash, going a slightly more normal color. "Was that you, Timmy boy?" Timothy, the boy with the Capability to control electrical items, gave him a thumbs-up.

Now, usually, if a man dressed in yellow and black appears above your school roof, feet balanced on the backs of two huge robot wasps, you would notice. But, in the middle of a savage assault course set by a maniac, you could easily miss it. And indeed most of the class did, as they concentrated instead on tackling the second obstacle, a wide ditch that you had to swing across using ropes. Except the ropes were on fire.

Nektar looked down across the field, scanning for likely targets as he spoke into his remote control: "Attack

drones, engage mind-
control helmets.
Prepare for combat
and assimilation."

A hatch
toward the
back of each
of the four
drones
opened,

and four of Knox's yellow
helmets were lowered into attack position.

His earpiece crackled: "Focus on the teacher first,
Lord Nektar," said Knox's voice. "He is quite an impressive
specimen. The man with the large mustache by the
wooden building."

Nektar saw Mr. Flash at once: he was standing
alone by the shed, bellowing something to Elsa
about freezing the rope and leaving everyone else
behind.

Nektar spoke into his attack drone control unit: "Target
the shouting bald man to our right. Capture him!"

Before Mr. Flash, or indeed anyone else, had noticed what was happening, one of the drones was hovering above him. A yellow helmet was lowered onto his head, and his shouting stopped abruptly as the lights along the sides of it winked on. Mr. Flash's eyes emptied, then went a frightening pattern of black and yellow.

"Welcome to the hive, my friend," murmured Nektar, who had landed beside him.

"That's bees, Lord Nektar," said Knox's voice in his ear, but Nektar ignored it. Instead, he had some instructions for Mr. Flash.

"You are now servant to Lord Nektar, human drone. And you will help me to conquer and capture everyone at this school."

"I obey, Lord Nektar," said Mr. Flash in a monotone.

"Begin with the most powerful. Who else has a power like yours, human drone?" demanded Nektar as a hula hoop skimmed past them.

"The Sheriff has my power," said the teacher, pointing at Dirk Scott, who had reappeared behind the youngest students to prod them toward the burning ropes.

But just then, Dirk looked back over his shoulder and saw what was going on. He took in Mr. Flash, with his blank eyes, and the weirdly costumed man by his side who seemed to be giving him instructions. This didn't look good. As an attack drone whizzed toward him, already lowering a helmet, Dirk raced into action.

"Debs, get the HALO unit, we've got to warn the Alliance!" he shouted as he sprinted with superhuman speed across the field toward his friend. He glanced back over his shoulder to check the position of the attack drones. Two were following him. As he reached the edge of the woods, he looked around: "Debs!"

"You will be a servant of Lord Nektar," droned the voice of Deborah Lamington, and before Dirk could move, a rope had been thrown around him, pinning his arms to his sides.

Deborah walked around to face him. She wore a yellow helmet fixed over her dark hair; her eyes were wide and staring, their whites an eerie yellow with a jet-black center.

"Embrace your destiny," she hissed at him. "Join us."

Dirk was powerless. An attack wasp lowered a helmet over his head and he, too, became a helpless servant.

With Mr. Flash and the Posse on his side, Nektar had rapidly gained the upper hand. He had two fully operational Heroes, backed up by four huge, heavily armed drones. Mr. Souperman's super-strength could have presented a problem, but Deborah's first action after trapping Dirk was to grab a large stone lying on the ground and throw it. It rose in an elegant arc above The School, then curved back on itself like a boomerang until it landed with a nasty-sounding crack on the side of the headmaster's head. He collapsed like a sack of onions dropped by a clumsy onion-sack-carrier.

Hemmed in by the huge attack drones, and up against such powerful foes, the rest of The School didn't have much time to plan a counterattack. A few tried to run but were quickly headed off by Dirk or Mr. Flash, who were easily able to overtake them and shove them back. Within five terrifying minutes it was over—students and teachers herded together at gunpoint, like apprehensive sheep, in front of the shed.

"Just in case anyone gets any more clever ideas, watch carefully . . . ," threatened Nektar, pointing to the row of dummies at the front of the assault course. "Attack drones, eliminate!"

The noise of the drones' engines changed pitch as they wheeled around in the air, and with a deafening clatter they opened fire. Straw flew in all directions as bullets ripped the figures apart. A huge roar followed as one of the drones fired a huge jet of flame across the whole scene, reducing the dummies to a row of blackened, charred poles.

Everyone decided at the same moment that it might not be the right time to be a Hero.

As the last bits of straw fluttered to the ground, Nektar shouted peevishly, "I know, I know. You don't have to keep nagging me."

Several people turned to look at him quizzically.

"I wasn't talking to you, prisoners!" he snapped at them.

In fact, he'd been talking to Nicholas Knox, who kept reminding him in his ear that he needed to select the best candidates to mind-control, then clear out with the rest of his prisoners before the police arrived.

But Nektar was reluctant to rush home. If we're honest, he was enjoying having some independence for once; it was surprisingly nice to be out and about capturing people and burning stuff instead of being cooped up in his lair with Knox trying to upstage him all the time.

Ah well, he thought to himself, *no rest for the wicked. I HATE PICNICS.*

"You!" he snapped at Mr. Flash. "Bald human drone!"

"I am ready to serve, master," intoned Mr. Flash.

"Identify the strongest and most powerful candidates for mind control," ordered Nektar. "The rest will be imprisoned until we can build more mind-control helmets and add them to the army."

"These students show potential," replied Mr. Flash, indicating Gangly Fuzz Face and his four misshapen cohorts.

Before they could protest, the Posse cornered them as mind-control helmets were lowered onto their heads.

"This teacher is a former Hero known as the Weasel," revealed Mr. Flash. Mr. Drench was hauled out of the crowd and his eyes too became staring yellow-and-black orbs.

"Police have left their station house to respond to reports of explosions, mighty Nektar," Mr. Drench-drone informed his new master. "They will arrive here in approximately four minutes. No, wait . . ." He cocked his head and listened intently: "Four minutes and forty-eight seconds. I just heard a traffic light go red."

"Right," fussed Nektar. "Knox, how many mind-control helmets do we have left?"

"Four, sir," crackled Knox in his ear. "And I do suggest you hurry."

Why does he insist on patronizing me? thought Nektar. *I HATE PICNICS.*

"Um, okay, attack drones, mind-control the following people," he ordered, beginning to feel slightly panicky, like when you're late for a train or something and the tops of your legs go all weird. He scanned the crowd for victims and his insect eyes rested on four figures conveniently huddled together over to one side.

"Those four. Take them," instructed Nektar, flailing a finger in the direction of Mary, Billy, Nellie, and Hilda. Billy whimpered in panic, inadvertently inflating his left elbow.

Pork Belly, who was closest to them, chimed in. "They are of no operational use, mighty Lord Nektar. These children are referred to as the Super Zeroes because of their weakness and lack of potential."

"All right, all right," said a panicked Nektar: *What is the point of a mind-controlled army—I HATE PICNICS—*he thought to himself, *if they start arguing back?* "That large boy over there, then. He looks hefty," he continued, now picking people out almost at random. "And, oh, I don't know . . . those three," indicating some muscly-looking final year students.

And with that, four final pairs of eyes morphed into glazed yellow-and-black pools, and Nektar's attack was complete. His servants began herding everyone around to the front of The School, and Mr. Flash brought up the rear, carrying the still-unconscious Mr. Souperman over his shoulder.

The trucks were standing ready with their back doors open and their engines running.

"All prisoners into the vehicles at once," ordered Nektar sharply. "Attack drones, prepare to destroy on sight anyone who tries to run or fight back. *Oooh, look at the tiny horses!"*

Everyone immediately turned to look at the two small

white horses that were cantering across the schoolyard, tossing their miniature manes and clopping their delicate hooves in an impressive display of small-scale dressage. The prisoners watched out of simple curiosity; Nektar's human servants and even his robotic attack and spy drones all looked because he had just ordered them to.

After a final canter, the horses disappeared with a tiny **neigh**. Everyone went **"Awwww!"** in a disappointed way.

"Right, into the vehicles then, come on!" Nektar ordered, and the prisoners were pushed and pulled and threatened into the back of the trucks. The attack drones locked themselves onto their specially adapted racks on the top of each of the four vehicles. The spy drones whirred into the sky and headed back to base.

Doors slammed, tires screeched, and within moments the schoolyard was empty. There were no witnesses around to read the words "Ribbon Robotics" on the trucks that roared away down the road.

Nor was there anyone around to see the four small figures who floated back down to earth a few seconds later, all clinging tightly to the handle of a single yellow umbrella.

19

Murph Alone

A mile away, oblivious to the dramatic events unfolding at his soon-to-be ex-school, Murph was grumpy. Really grumpy. In fact, if you saw him, you'd go as far as to say he was full-on Grumpelstiltskin. Everything was annoying him. Fed up doesn't even start to cover it. He'd arrived back home, slung his bag down on the floor, and flopped onto the sofa.

To add to his annoyance, a wasp was buzzing around. Eventually Murph succeeded in batting it out of the window. This reminded him of Carl, which in turn made him feel bad for avoiding him today. But Murph was simply in one of those unavoidable funks.

It wouldn't have improved Murph's mood to know that, not far away, Nicholas Knox had been watching him via the spy drone that Murph had just dealt with. Knox didn't want any witnesses to his plans—and he couldn't be sure that Murph hadn't seen the words "Ribbon Robotics" on the trucks that had passed him on their way into The School. He was a loose end, and Knox hated loose ends.

He leaned forward and spoke quietly into his microphone. "Attack drone 4, this is an emergency override, code 24. Proceed to the location of Spy Drone 260 and obliterate the human target. Activate."

On the top of the trucks now speeding toward the factory, one of the large attack drones buzzed into life. It detached itself from its special rack and flew off on its deadly mission.

Back at his house, Murph was following the rules of dealing with a bad mood. If you're not aware of these rules, here's a handy guide for the next time you're feeling rotten:

Things to Do When You're in a Funk:
1. First of all, it's important to embrace it. BE the grump. As long as you're not rude to people, it

can be quite fun. Enjoy the feeling of being a moody old so-and-so for a bit.

2. Eat. You must eat plenty of treats to fill up the happiness tank.

3. Drink. Fill up your belly with soda.

4. Listen to sad music. If possible use headphones, go for a walk in the rain, and pretend that you're in a sad movie about your own life and this is the soundtrack.

Murph had made himself a bowl of the sugariest cereal he could find (Rule 2) and settled down on the sofa, reaching for the remote control for the music system. Time for Rule 4. Mournful piano music began. He was ready to immerse himself in *Wronged Murph—The Movie*.

"*Hello—*" the singer began.

BANG!

"*It's me—*"

SMASH!

Murph jerked his head toward the staircase. The almighty noise had come from upstairs.

He jumped off the sofa, milk and sugary flakes leaping out of the bowl and onto the floor as he did so. His heart was racing.

"What on earth was that?" he said out loud to try and calm himself down. It didn't work.

Maybe he was imagining things, he thought, though more out of hope than anything else. He just wanted a quiet afternoon listening to music and feeling sorry for himself.

His hope was dashed as soon as he heard another **BANG!** followed by the tinkling of glass.

Murph crept over to the staircase and slowly started to climb. He had never noticed the stairs creaking before, but now that he was on full alert they seemed to have become the world's loudest steps. What was up there?

As he reached the middle of the staircase, he heard a distant buzzing sound. He stopped dead in his tracks, frozen to the stairs like someone doing a lame impression of Spider-Man.

There was silence. An eerie silence. Time stood still for a moment . . .

And then there was a sudden roar that seemed to tear the air around him to shreds. With a cold splash of shock, Murph realized that the staircase *actually was* being torn to shreds. He was being shot at!

He threw himself blindly to one side as something flew at him with incredible speed, firing as it went. Trinkets and figurines downstairs dinged and clattered as they were shot to pieces.

Murph rushed up the stairs and at the top hopped behind the laundry basket on the landing. He peered cautiously over the top. Hovering just above the floor down by the front door was a giant wasp. Wisps of smoke rose from the gun barrels mounted on either side.

The drone seemed to be collecting itself, ready for another attack run. Before it had a chance to move, Murph left the safe haven of the basket, dashed to his bedroom, and shut the door. He needed a plan.

On the plus side, this was a home game for Murph. He figured that he had a slight advantage because he knew the layout of his house. *You* may argue that the fire-breathing attack wasp with powerful mounted machine guns also had a fair shot at this battle, but the years of moving and making and losing friends had made Murph Cooper pretty unflappable.

He could now hear the drone outside his bedroom door, hovering, thinking about what to do next. A couple of times it let off a salvo of gunfire, as if this would encourage Murph to come out. The door shook as bullets thudded into it.

What it *did* encourage Murph to do was open his window and prepare to escape. But before he could figure out his next move, the drone lost patience and began burning his bedroom door down. Smoke billowed in. He knew he had seconds to get out.

He grabbed the baseball bat he'd been given for Christmas, climbed onto the window ledge, and began to shimmy down the bathroom drainpipe. He started slowly, inching down with his hands and trying to cling on with his feet, until he realized he was losing his grip and couldn't proceed at this rate. He had no choice but to freefall. Luckily it wasn't that far off the ground when his fingers decided to give up, and he landed neatly in one of his mom's shrubs, squashing a large purple plant.

She'll shout at me for that, he thought, then remembered that his bedroom door was on fire and that maybe shrubs wouldn't be a priority. Even purple ones.

Murph picked himself up and darted around to the front door of the house. Slowly and silently, he opened it.

The house was starting to fill with smoke; Murph could hear the crackle of burning wood upstairs, but he couldn't see or hear his enemy. He needed to make it to the kitchen, which had two different doors to the outside, so if things went wrong he would be able to escape through one of them. He assumed the drone was upstairs, still trying to burst into his bedroom.

He assumed wrongly.

The drone *had* burst into his bedroom, but what Murph didn't realize was that it had quietly tracked him all the way outside and was now hovering behind his head, the buzz of its rotors covered by the crackle of the spreading flames now visible at the top of the stairs.

As he started to creep across the living room, Murph froze.

He knew something was wrong—and suddenly he registered the tickle of a light breeze on his neck. His fingers flexed on the handle of the baseball bat, and in one quick, sharp movement he raised the bat up and over his head as if he were using an ax in reverse, smacking the drone off target seconds before it opened fire.

Machine guns roared as the giant attack wasp flailed across the room, rotors whining frantically as it tried to correct its spin. Bullets sprayed everywhere—pinging off the mirror, thunking into the sofa, and smashing the stereo.

Murph's eyes fell on the jumble of rain boots just inside the front door, and he remembered he'd hidden the Grapple Gun in one of them. As the drone tried to get itself back under control, he rummaged frantically inside the boots, ending up with quite a smelly left hand but also, eventually, the gun. Just as the drone took aim at him for its final, deadly assault, Murph pulled the trigger. The hook exploded out across the room and into the kitchen, smashing into the oven door and wrapping itself around the handle. Murph pressed the button on the butt of the gun and was catapulted into the kitchen as the grappling line reeled itself in at speed.

He impressed himself by landing safely by the oven, silently thanking Carl as he did. Murph dropped the Grapple Gun and started to look around for a weapon.

As the drone appeared in the doorway, he threw everything he could get his hands on at it. Rolling pin, **BOOM!** Pot, **CLATTER!** Saucepans, **TING! SPLANG! DONG!**

His mom's favorite wok, **PANG!** (That was the biggest one.)

A small part of him was actually enjoying this, but another, much larger part was panicking: he was running out of utensils.

Suddenly a thought occurred to his frantic, battle-sharpened brain. If he could stop this thing flying around, surely he'd have a chance at nailing it . . .

He went to the windowsill, where his mom kept a classic mom item: a bowl of interesting stones that she'd brought back from a day at the beach the previous summer. (Scientists have tried, but failed, to explain why some moms do this; stones are among the many items you can put under the umbrella of "Mom Things," along with Native American dream catchers, delicate porcelain swans, and 37 percent more tissues than could ever realistically be required by a human.)

Anyway, back to the action.

Murph grabbed a handful of beach stones.

"Come and get me!" he taunted.

Guns blazing, the machine flew fast at his head, but Murph was ready. He flung himself onto the tiled kitchen floor. As the drone's momentum carried it above his head, Murph hurled the stones upward—and with a clang, a splutter, and a ping, its blades shattered.

The drone fell from the air and smashed into the ground behind the metal kitchen trash can. Sparks, debris, and five-day-old tea bags went everywhere. Then, blissful silence.

Murph had managed to restore order. He was very pleased with his action-packed last half an hour on earth.

"Phew," he breathed.

He wandered dazedly out of the kitchen and began staggering around the place. It didn't look like his house anymore. All the pictures were askew, the TV was smashed, and there were bullet holes and broken glass strewn everywhere. Smoke billowed down the stairs, blocking off the hallway completely.

What in the blue heck is going on? thought Murph to himself, finally. *What WAS that thing?* One thing was certain: the boring house had just become the venue for one of the least boring episodes in Murph's life.

He decided to take a few moments to compose himself and work out what he'd tell his mom. But before he could begin to start thinking of an excuse, a noise started that made the hairs on the back of his neck stand up—and, in fact, the hairs on the front of his neck too, which he hadn't even realized were there. It was a sinister, high-pitched whine, as the damaged drone rose slowly out from behind the trash can, supported by a set of reserve blades that had emerged from a hatch on its back.

The drone had a plan B. Murph did not.

Helplessly he watched as the guns, which had been knocked out of position, swiveled around until the barrels were pointing right at him.

This was the end.

At least Murph thought it was, right up until he saw a figure holding what looked like an unopened umbrella creep through the back door of the kitchen.

Mary rushed up behind the drone. There was a loud crack and a whirring sound like a crashing helicopter as she shoved her umbrella into the reserve blade. The drone spun frantically around, lurching drunkenly across the kitchen. In desperation it activated its flamethrower and spewed fire in a wide circle, like an extremely expensive and dangerous firework. With a metallic clang, it careered through the smashed door of the oven, which immediately filled with flames. After a moment there was a huge explosion. The drone, consumed by its own firepower, was reduced to spare parts. There would be no way back this time. It was done for.

"Murph?" yelled Mary. "Are you there?" Murph could just make her out through the smoke, and beyond that he could see Hilda, Nellie, and Billy watching nervously from the doorway.

"Over here!" shouted Murph, crawling underneath the thick smoke that was now filling the kitchen. "I'm over here, and I appear to be fine! What the salad is going on? What WAS that?"

Choking, the five of them staggered out through the back door and stood in the garden. Murph looked around, still baffled by what had just happened and what his pals were doing there. Mary tried to put into words the current state of affairs and couldn't. So they just continued to stand there and take stock. Billy eventually interrupted the silence.

"So. Here's the deal," he told Murph. "The School's been taken over by an evil wasp man and everyone's been imprisoned or brainwashed. Teachers too. Everyone except us."

"What? What do you mean, a 'wasp man'?" replied Murph.

"We don't really know," said Hilda. "He's just weird and waspy and his weapons are all wasps and it's all nuts, but he means business and he's got a lot of helpers. One of which you just managed to finish off in the kitchen."

"With the help of my umbrella," chipped in Mary, as she checked it for damage.

Murph took a final look back at his house. It was a complete wreck. Flames were licking out of the first-floor windows, and at that moment there was another explosion from the kitchen. He had no idea how he was going to explain this to his mom, but there was no time to worry about that right now.

Murph Cooper had been through a lot. But he'd had enough of feeling miserable; he was fed up with being fed up. He thought about what Mary had said to him only that morning—about not letting things get to you. Then he remembered something Flora had told him during one of their morning chess sessions: no one except a hedgehog ever got anywhere by rolling into a ball.

Murph wasn't a hedgehog, and it was time to take control of the situation. Even though Mr. Flash had done his best to beat any joy out of him, even though he was fated to leave in a few weeks, he liked The School. And even though he'd been a total jerk to his friends earlier that day, they had rushed to save him. For the first time in years, he felt part of something.

"We need to save The School," Murph stated simply.

"But, Murph, I don't know how we can do that," said Mary anxiously. "We're not super enough. We need a Hero, and we haven't got one. Who can help us now?"

And suddenly Murph understood. It was Mary's question that had been the key: Who could help them now?

Only one person. Someone who had not been seen for a very, very long time.

"Where are we going, Murph?" shouted Billy as they sprinted through the town center.

"Hurry up," Murph panted. "Back to The School before it's too late!"

Minutes later they tore through the gates and across the front yard. Murph led them around the back and across the playing fields. The empty assault course lay to one side, but over by the woods a stream of smoke could be seen coming out of the chimney on top of a ramshackle collection of wooden sheds. They could hear a metallic hammering coming from inside.

"He's stayed close by but didn't want anyone to know," puffed Murph as they ran. "He's got the equipment; he knows too much to be just a janitor. I only just worked it out for sure. Carl is the answer!"

"What?" said Mary as they stopped outside the huts, gasping for breath. "How can Carl help? How can Carl save us?"

"He's not just Carl," said Murph triumphantly. "He's the Blue Phantom."

The others looked at him in amazement. Then they did a collective **"Ohhhhhhh!"**

Murph nodded, turned, and knocked on the door of the shed. The clanging noise stopped abruptly.

Carl opened the door slowly: "Oh, it's you guys! Thank goodness you're safe. And what the heck are you doing back here? It's far too dangerous for little mice like you to be running around."

"We've come to save The School, and you're the only one who can help," Murph said earnestly.

"Me?" laughed Carl. "What am I going to do? Grab my broom and brush the bad guys away?"

"No, Carl. We know who you are. The game's up," said Mary confidently.

"We know your secret," chirped Hilda.

"Oh, do you?" said Carl.

"Yes. Yes, we do," piped up Billy, partially inflating his left thigh with nervous excitement.

Even Nellie got carried away in the moment and skitted around silently like a dog who knows it's about to go for a walkie.

Carl waited, holding the door half closed, eyebrows raised.

"You are the Blue Phantom," said Murph simply.

There was a pause, and then Carl let out a wheeze that turned out to be laughter.

"Brilliant. Well, I've heard it all now. Sorry, kids, not me!" he said. "Now, you'd better get yourselves home. It's not safe here for the likes of you."

And he slammed the door in their faces.

Murph couldn't even look at his friends. How could he have been so wrong? He'd been certain he'd worked it out.

"It must be him. It just doesn't make sense," he murmured, deflated.

"But you heard it from his own mouth," said Mary gently. "He isn't the Blue Phantom."

"Well, who is, then?" Hilda breathed.

Nobody said anything for a moment, and then an unexpected voice broke in from behind them.

"I am the Blue Phantom," said the voice.

THE END

Okay—not the end. But things are quite exciting at the moment, so we thought it might be a good idea to break the tension. Let's all calm down for a minute with a nice story about a rabbit, shall we?

Interlude:
The Tale of Alan Rabbit

Alan Rabbit gamboled up to the top of the hill and looked out over the meadow. The morning sun was just rising above the hedges, and all the world seemed new.

Alan twitched his little rabbit nose: twitch, twitch. Then he wiggled his little rabbit tail and began singing a song that went *"Uh-huh, oh yeah, shake your rabbit booty."*

Just then his phone rang.

"Hello," said Alan Rabbit into

the phone. "Yes, Mom. Yes, I'll be there in a minute."

Now, Old Mrs. Pollyanna Rabbit was a most particular rabbit. She kept their sandy rabbit hole spotlessly clean and was quite put out if houseguests made a mess.

Only the other day, Mr. Pobbletoes, the death metal badger, had made an awful commotion in the scullery, smashing the television and smearing chocolate sauce up the walls.

"I do declare, I am quite distracted," Mrs. Pollyanna Rabbit had bemoaned, surveying the damage and calling him a taxi.

She had only just this very morning finished getting everything back in order.

Alan Rabbit bounced back into the rabbit hole, simply covered with dew and good vibes. "What's for breakfast, Mother?" he asked.

"I've made your favorite," Mrs. Rabbit said with a smile, "avocado on sourdough toast. It's all ready for you in the scullery."

"What is a scullery, Mother?" asked Alan Rabbit as he dug into his delicious repast.

"Hush now, tish and patootie," scolded his mother. "Eat your breakfast, and I shall sing you your favorite song."

"The one about the otters?" asked Alan Rabbit excitedly.

"Yes," soothed Old Mrs. Pollyanna Rabbit. And then she sang him this song about otters, which you must make up a tune for. Just reading the words is not acceptable.

Old Mrs. Pollyanna Rabbit's Otter Song

Baby otters, baby otters,
Rolling in the sun.
Baby otters, baby otters,
Having lots of fun.
See them gambol, see them play,
See them take a pee.
Baby otters, baby otters,
What will they grow up to be?
Adult otters, probably.

Ah, that's better. Feeling calmer?

Right, where were we? Ah yes . . . a voice behind them just said something really exciting.

20

Flight of the Super Zeroes

"**I am the Blue Phantom,**" said the voice behind them.

The five friends spun around on the spot with their mouths open, a display that would have earned them perfect marks if synchronized surprise were an event at the Olympics.

Standing behind them was a slender figure in blue armor, casting a huge, dramatic shadow back over the deserted and, in places, still-smoking playing fields. The figure reached up and removed a sleek blue helmet, revealing the beaming face and fluffy hair of Flora, the headmaster's secretary. "Hadn't figured that one out, had you?" she asked them delightedly.

Murph rolled his eyes. His day could not get any weirder. But, as he'd learned by now, sometimes it's best to just go with the flow. So he did.

"You're the legendary Blue Phantom?" he asked.

"Oh, I don't know about 'legendary,'" replied Flora modestly.

"Who are *you*, then?" said Mary, turning to Carl, who had reopened his door and was staring at Flora with his eyebrows raised.

"Yeah," added Murph. "Why is there a photo of you and Captain Alpha in your shed?"

"Are you a Hero too? What's your Cape?" Hilda wanted to know.

"I don't have a Cape," replied Carl gruffly. "I was the only one here without one until Kid Normal came along."

"But the Blue Phantom wouldn't have gotten very far without him," added Flora kindly. "Who do you think built my car? And invented my armor?

And who do you think designed that HALO unit they're still using, eh?"

"What, the thing that looks like a cell phone?" asked Murph.

Carl and Flora both laughed.

"That unit was around a long time before cell phones," she told him.

"So, you're what? Her sidekick?" asked Hilda.

"Yeah, if you like. *Sidekick*," said Carl, not sounding as if he was too keen on the word. "I prefer 'husband,' but yeah, 'sidekick' if you like." He turned and disappeared back into his workshop, calling over his shoulder to Flora as he did so, "What do you want to do with these folks, then?"

"We could do with all the help we can get on this one, I reckon," she replied.

Carl didn't answer, but they could hear rattling noises and a door creaking.

The Super Zeroes turned back to the Blue Phantom.

"So . . . you used to swoop in and save the day when all hope was lost?" asked Hilda.

"Well, yes, that was the general idea," replied Flora.

"Are you . . . are you still available to do that?" inquired Billy hopefully.

"Well, it's been quite a while, dear. The world has changed. You can't go saving anyone these days without someone shoving a camera in your face. Back in the old days, I just used to track down the bad guys and kick them in the face. Nowadays you're a scandal on the news! Oh, and the risk assessments you have to do! I haven't got time for risk assessments. I'm the Blue Phantom," Flora pointed out, "not the regional manager of a shoe store."

Murph wondered if this was the real reason that nobody had seen the Blue Phantom for so long. But there wasn't time for that right now. He stepped forward:

"Well, I haven't got a camera phone. My mom won't let me. But we do need to save our school, and you know what? Only the Blue Phantom can help us now."

In the background, Carl dropped an oilcan as if to punctuate Murph's movie-like declaration. It added to the drama of the moment and gave Murph and the rest of the gang a little shiver.

"Well, I could never say no to that line," smiled Flora. "Come on, then," she called through the open shed door to Carl, "fire her up!"

"Fire what up?" said Murph. "You don't mean . . ."

He was interrupted by the whine of jet engines from the larger building to the side of Carl's workshop. The double doors that had always been locked tight shuddered and then burst open. A plume of smoke and dust billowed out, and when it cleared, a bullet-shaped silvery-blue object emerged.

With a deep purr from the engines, the Blue Phantom's car gracefully rolled out into the afternoon light, its four enormous black tires hissing as they ate up the tarmac in front of them and the jet engines making a haze in the still air.

"We call her the *Banshee*," said the Blue Phantom proudly, "and she's not taken us on a mission in thirty-five years. Nothing to worry about, though . . . just means she's well rested, eh, Carl?"

They all looked inside the *Banshee* to see Carl in the cockpit, chuckling to himself. "She's been well looked after, dearest," he added happily.

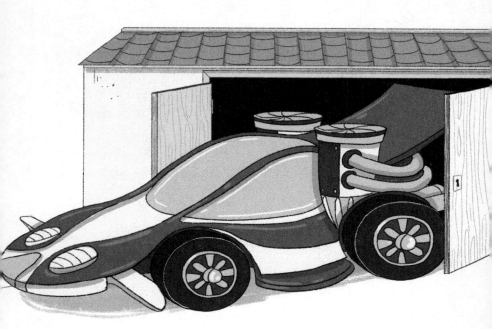

"You mean this has been in that shed the whole time? I've been sweeping up leaves right next to the world's coolest car, and you didn't think to say something?" sputtered Murph.

"Well, those leaves weren't going to tidy themselves, and I needed to keep you focused. You had to live up to your name. Isn't that right, Captain Brush?" Carl gave a wheezy chuckle. "And incidentally, this school isn't going to save itself either. So we can all stand around here chatting like old hens, or we can jump into the *Banshee* and save the day."

Everyone was a big fan of the second option by this stage, and began to work out how to get in. The front seat was Flora's spot—it seemed only right considering it was her car—and she was in there like a flash. Or more accurately, a phantom. A quick double somersault, a forward dive, and she was ready to go. Mightily impressive it was, too.

"Pilates," she explained. "Keeps you wonderfully supple."

The *Banshee* didn't have much in the way of a back seat, but there was an area behind the twin pilots' chairs where Murph and the four other Super Zeroes squashed themselves in.

The inside of the jet car smelled of leather and oil; the floor was metal. In front of them Carl was flicking switches on a wide control panel that was covered with exciting colored lights. With a hiss of hydraulics, the doors closed, sealing them all inside the shiny capsule.

"Off we go, then!" cried Flora chirpily.

"That's it?" blurted Murph.

"What do you mean, dear?" asked Flora, turning around.

"Well, haven't you got a really cool catchphrase for when you launch your jet-powered car?"

"Yeah," piped up Billy.

"Well, what do you suggest, Billy?" asked Flora.

"Oh, I don't know." He panicked. He hadn't thought of an alternative. "Ummm, something like . . . *'BANSHEE-A-GO-GO'*?"

Everyone laughed. Billy's head swelled with embarrassment.

"Let's stick with 'Off we go, then', then," decided Murph.

"Right, hold on!" Flora turned back to Carl and said matter-of-factly, **"Off we go, then."**

There was a clunk, a whizz, and a ping, which was mildly exciting. Then suddenly a humongous roar, which was very exciting indeed. They were all pressed down into the floor as the *Banshee* shot into the sky.

"Ribbon Robotics, you said, Murph?" shouted Carl over the noise of the jets. "That's over on the other side of town. I know it. Doesn't look like great conditions for us, though," he muttered, consulting the control panel in front of him.

"I don't know what you're talking about," piped up Hilda. "It's turning into a lovely evening, perfect for a picnic or a little horsey ride or, you know, flying around in a jet car."

"Not in a *secret* jet car, though," Carl told her. "Everyone in town is going to see us. We need to find cover."

"I can help!" said a muffled voice from underneath Murph's leg.

It wasn't a voice he recognized. Shocked, he realized that it had come from a very squashed Nellie.

Nellie muscled her way out from under the aforementioned Murph-leg, or leg of Murph, and squeezed herself in between Flora and Carl at the front of the cockpit. Then she screwed her face up in concentration.

Almost immediately, a layer of thin white cloud began to appear below the hovering *Banshee*, spreading out like ripples on a pond to cover the whole town.

"Wonderful work, dear!" exclaimed Flora. "Is this the first time you've used your Cape in a real situation?"

"Yes, Your Majesty," said Nellie in a panic.

Flora laughed kindly and ruffled her hair. "Well, you've done remarkably well. Thank you."

Carl reached over to the control panel and pulled a lever. They heard a whirring noise as the jet engines rotated and the *Banshee* shot forward across the sheet of concealing cloud.

Mary wanted some in-flight information. "So if you're the Blue Phantom . . . ," she began.

"I think we covered that," murmured Murph.

Mary shushed him. "Then who runs The School, you or Mr. Souperman?"

"Well." Flora considered this question. "We all set it up together, really. Geoffrey looks after day-to-day matters. But I certainly keep an eye on things. After all, Murph, who do you think suggested to him that you should stay at The School?"

"Why did you want me to stay?" Murph asked.

"Oh, well, I've always had a soft spot for the boy without a Cape, you know," said Flora, reaching over and squeezing Carl's hand. "And you looked so miserable sitting there that day. Poor little mite. Anyway . . ." She peered out of the windshield. "It's a left turn here, isn't it, dear?"

"Oh, don't start all that again. It's one thing I *haven't*

missed in the last thirty-five years," grumbled Carl. "I know what I'm doing and I know where I'm going. Leave me alone."

"All I'm saying is there's nothing wrong with stopping to ask directions every once in a while," said Flora.

"Look. I got lost ONCE, when we were combatting the Mongoose in '74. And even then, asking for directions was more trouble than it was worth. Remember trying to explain that one away? 'Oh, sorry, officer, do you know where we can find the Mongoose? Me and my wife, the Blue Phantom, seem to have gotten lost in our FLYING JET CAR!' Anyway, look, I'm not going to get lost."

Carl pointed to a screen in the center of the main panel in front of him.

"GPS," he declared proudly. "I've made a lot of special modifications myself." He gave them all a wink.

"Can we stop to pee, please?" asked Billy.

"Save the world first. Pee later," replied Flora. "Page one of the *Spy Handbook*, if you must know. I remember someone telling me that once. Anyway, do you think it's time to have a quick run-through of your plan? We'll be there in a couple of minutes; it says so here on Carl's newfangled hoojamaflip."

"Plan?" said Murph, Hilda, Mary, Billy, and even Nellie.

"We were kind of hoping you'd be able to help us out with that," Mary added, embarrassed.

"Well," said Flora, "this Nektar sounds like a nasty piece of work. And he's got some of the most powerful weaponry I've ever heard about. But what I think I'd do is—"

Before she could impart her wisdom, there was a huge **BANG** and a sudden rushing of wind as the glass beside her shattered. A bullet had pinged across the metal cabin, denting the wall behind them.

Outside the window was the hovering yellow-and-black shape of one of Nektar's attack drones.

Flora didn't seem unduly worried. "We've got company, Carl," she said calmly.

"This was always my favorite part," said Carl with a grin, and he jerked his control wheel sharply to the right. "Hang on!" he shouted as he pulled the *Banshee* into a sideslip, leaving the drone behind as they dropped toward the thin cloud layer still shimmering below them.

"Your destination is in three hundred yards," intoned a lady's calm voice from the dashboard.

But up ahead they could make out the shape of a second attack drone hovering just above the cloud cover and moving rapidly toward them. Tiny sparks appeared on each side of it, and with horror Murph realized that it was opening fire. Bullets pinged off the *Banshee*'s windscreen.

"I always said you should have made the side windows bulletproof as well," chided Flora.

"Now," said Carl through gritted teeth, pulling back on the controls and sending the vehicle spiraling upward and out of range, "is not the time for feedback. But thank you, dear, it's been noted. And if we survive this, I'll certainly look into it." He pushed on another lever to his right, and the engines increased in pitch. "Let's see if we can outrun 'em, at least." The *Banshee* shot forward.

"Your destination is in two hundred yards," the GPS lady informed everyone.

Hilda had her nose pressed to the window at the

back of the cabin. "I can see them. They're dropping behind," she shouted excitedly. "I think we're going to make it."

"How many of these big drones were there at The School?" asked Murph.

"Four," replied Mary. "We got rid of one at your house, then there are two more back there. That makes three, so . . . oh."

"Your destination is in one hundred yards."

"Carl, there's another one!" yelled Murph over the scream of the jets.

Carl turned his head: "What?"

"There's another . . . **LOOK OUT!"**

The fourth drone had broken the cloud cover just ahead and was flying straight toward them at full speed.

Flora turned to Carl, suddenly looking deadly serious. "Get these kids down safely," she urged him.

Carl looked back at her. "Don't worry, I will," he told her. "Never again, remember?" Flora nodded, and then vanished in a flash.

Within seconds, the drone was just yards away, aiming its machine guns at them through the broken side window.

But before it could fire, it suddenly lurched backward, bullets streaming harmlessly over the *Banshee*'s roof. Murph could just make out a bluish shimmer on its rear end. Flora was straddling the drone's back.

An invisible retiree riding a giant robot wasp, Murph thought to himself. *That's not something you see every day.*

The *Banshee* moved slightly to one side as the Blue Phantom grabbed onto the swinging passenger door, holding the attack drone tightly with its guns pointed upward so it couldn't fire at them.

"Carl, bring us down so I can finish this thing off!" they heard her yell over the scream of the engines.

Carl moved a lever to rotate the jets and bring the *Banshee* lower, but as they moved, the attack drone was sucked through the intake of the left-hand jet engine. The engine sputtered and sparked, giving out a cloud of smoke and flame. The *Banshee* veered sickeningly to one side and began to lose altitude. Flora was nowhere to be seen.

"We're going down!" shouted Carl unnecessarily. "Get ready to bail! Mary, you got that umbrella? Flora, where are you?" He touched a button in front of him, and with a whine of motors, a hatch behind them began to open.

Outside they could see nothing but Nellie's layer of cloud rushing past.

"We need to shift some weight." Carl yelled. **"Mary, get that umbrella up and get everyone on the ground!"**

"What about you?" screamed Mary as she looked at the umbrella, willing it to be okay again since it was used to see off the first attack drone.

"We'll be fine. This is your first time being shot down, am I right?"

"Um, . . . yes, oddly enough it is," she replied.

"Well, this is our hundredth. I told you, we'll be fine. We're tough old things. Get yourselves down there and get saving." Then Murph heard Carl mutter to himself,

"One hundred crash landings, eh? Do we get a letter from the queen?"

Flora's voice came from the roof: "I imagine we'll get one from the insurance company." And Carl smiled with relief that she was alive. But then there was another huge bang as the left-hand engine exploded. Smoke began to fill the cockpit.

"Jump," Carl ordered the five Super Zeroes. **"Now!"**

The last thing they heard before they leaped into white nothingness, holding Mary's umbrella handle for dear life, was the GPS saying, **"You have reached your destination."**

A few moments later there was an enormous crash and an explosion from somewhere to the right.

21

The Hot Dog Minute

The Super Zeroes floated gently toward the ground. Below them lay Ribbon Robotics, the tower at its far end casting a long shadow like a threatening, pointing finger.

The concrete area at the front of the factory was brightly lit by two huge floodlights. Five yellow dots near the entrance gave away the position of Nektar's new servants standing guard, but there seemed to be few other signs of life. There was no sound and no sign of the *Banshee*.

Mary started guiding them straight toward the building, but Murph hissed at her to change direction.

"No, Mary, that way, *that way*." He was pointing across the road from the main gates, where a closed-up food truck was parked. "Behind the food truck."

Mary changed course, and the five of them made

a soft landing on the road, shielded from any watching eyes in the factory by what they could now see was **Large John's Deluxe Snack Wagon**.

"Not an ideal time to stop for a hot dog, Murph, is it? And besides, they're closed," said Mary acidly.

"I don't want a hot dog, actually," Murph retorted, realizing that if there was one thing he really wanted right now, it was, in fact, a hot dog.

"But we can't just go barreling in there. We wouldn't stand a chance. We need a minute to work this out, right?"

The other four nodded. He was right.

"We could do this on

every mission, and call it 'Murph's Minute,'" said Hilda, liking the sound of it.

"Or 'Hot Dog Minute,'" suggested Billy.

"'Murph's Minute's better,'" said Mary.

"Can we focus, please," pleaded Murph. "Right, let's see where we're at. The *Banshee* has crashed."

Nellie let out a frightened sob.

"But there's nothing we can do about that now," said Murph gently. "It's not ideal that Flora and Carl aren't here right now, but maybe it's not only the Blue Phantom who can save us. Maybe we can do this ourselves." He paused. A brief pang of panic bolted through his belly as the magnitude of the task at hand dawned on him. For a moment even he was unconvinced by the words he was saying. But he pressed on, hoping that if *he* believed what he was saying, they would too. "We've got to try," he went on, puffing out his chest. "Right—what's the situation we're facing?"

"Evil man-wasp in factory," said Billy, surprisingly calmly. As he continued, he became less calm. "Um, plus mind-controlled Capability kids. And at least two mind-controlled teachers. And the rest of school is held captive! It's not looking good."

"It's okay, Billy. Deep breaths," Murph reassured him. "We can handle this. We just have to keep our heads. And keep them the same size," he joked, to defuse the tension. It worked. Billy let out a little chuckle as Murph continued. "So, what's our mission?"

Hilda piped up, "The wasp man must be stopped before he can take over the entire school and form a full mind-controlled army. We must storm the factory, defeat the hideous genetic hybrid, and save the day." Somehow she made it all sound quite matter-of-fact, using the same tone of voice she would normally use to say something like, "We must go to the meadow, pick some daisies, and make a delicate daisy chain to weave into my hair, tra la."

It was at this point that Murph realized the other four were looking at him expectantly but confidently. As if he was their leader or something. Another little pang of panic lurched in his stomach, but to disguise it he asked a third question.

"And what do we have on our side?"

"Flying," replied Mary, pointing at herself with the umbrella. "Ballooning," she went on slightly more uncertainly, indicating Billy. "Weather," she added, waving her other hand in Nellie's direction. "And, er, horses. Tiny horses," she concluded. Hilda stuck her thumbs up.

There was a moment of silence while they contemplated their powers and how they stacked up against heavily armed attack drones and powerful mind-controlled servants. It's a good thing no one had told them that the wasp man had stingers on his wrists.

"Bravery," said a voice suddenly. Nellie had raised her head and was pointing at Murph. "Doing the right thing. Not giving up. Seeing things other people don't see. Helping us work together. Staying positive."

"And blushing," added Mary as Murph's cheeks went full-on traffic-light red.

Murph wasn't sure he really had any of those powers. But he had made a decision back at his ruined house; he had decided to mount this rescue mission. And although it had been a long time since Murph Cooper had decided anything, once a choice was made he followed it through to the bitter end. His friends were relying on him.

"All right," he told his team, trying to look more confident than he felt, "huddle up. I think I know how we can do this."

Behind the food truck, Murph's Minute—or the Hot Dog Minute, if you prefer—concluded with a plan. "First thing," began Murph, wondering if rescue planning might turn out to be his Cape after all, "if we're going to sneak in there without anyone seeing us, we need to get those lights off . . ."

The reception desk at Ribbon Robotics was run by a woman named Patsy McLean. Nobody was quite sure how long she'd worked there, because nobody dared ask her. In fact, few people dared speak to her at all, because she was so incredibly rude and fierce. She had stiff black hair like a stuffed raven and a mean, pinched face that made her look like the sort of person who might actually grab a passing raven and stuff it—without even asking nicely first.

Patsy sat in the building's most comfortable chair, which she had insisted on getting because she falsely claimed to have a bad back. She tapped away at her computer, sending staff members aggressive e-mails about tidying up their coffee cups at the end of the day. And she hated absolutely everybody except her cat, Boris.

Patsy McLean was unaware that the building had been taken over by a crazed genetic hybrid with an evil plan to take over the country. When a man in a yellow jumpsuit had led a large group of  people through her reception area earlier that day, at gunpoint and with the help of three armored drones, she hadn't asked questions. His security pass was valid, and that was all she cared about.

A little later on, after all the rest of the staff had been sent home, five children with black-and-yellow eyes had marched back through the reception area and taken up guard positions outside. But Patsy had been busy composing a particularly unkind all-staff e-mail about the state of the bathrooms on the first floor. And besides, she was due to go home soon—she wasn't too bothered about the human drones unless they left a coffee cup lying around, in which case they were in real trouble.

Upstairs on the fourth floor, Gary, the work-experience intern, gazed out the boardroom windows overlooking the back of the building. The lights had come on as a layer of unexpected cloud had rolled in across the sky at the end of the day, and dusk had arrived early.

It's going to be a lovely sunset, he thought poetically, trying to ignore the fact that the rest of the room was so weird-looking.

The doors to the boardroom were guarded by several human drones in yellow helmets. Their black-and-yellow eyes gave Gary the creeps. The two remaining attack drones had landed on a table to one side, where they were recharging at a wall socket. And not far away from him, near the main windows looking out over the front of the building, Nektar and Nicholas Knox were talking urgently in low voices.

Brainwashed servants, thought Gary, *small helicopters with flamethrowers, evil wasp guy. Yep—best just to concentrate on the sunset.* His best friend from college was doing an internship at a chicken restaurant and was allowed free spicy wings at the end of the day. Gary very much felt that he had drawn the short straw.

"Spy drones indicate that the vehicle crashed somewhere off to the east," Knox was saying.

"Which way is that?" buzzed Nektar petulantly. He hated it when people talked about things happening to the east—or, in fact, any point of the compass—because he could never work out which way they meant. Mentally he spelled out the word N-E-W-S but then realized he didn't know which way north was, so it was absolutely no help.

"Over there, sir, just where you can see that large plume of smoke," said Knox oilily. "I have sent spy drones to establish who the intruders were, but I surmise that word of our attack on The School has been picked up somehow by other people with similar . . . abilities."

Nektar nodded intelligently, wondering what "surmise" meant. There was a loud crack of thunder from outside, and a couple of fat raindrops slapped against the windows.

"I will go and garner drone reports with which to update you," continued Knox, "but I suggest we prepare the facility for possible infiltration."

Just then all the lights fizzed, flickered, and went out,

as if they were voice-controlled and the signal to turn off was the word "infiltration." But that would have been odd. Yellowish emergency lights turned on, mingling with the brownish-orange light from the thundery late afternoon sky outside to give the room an unpleasant glow.

Nektar looked around in a jittery way, like a panicked wasp in a glass bottle.

"I'm going to my tower, Knox," he said nervously. "Keep me updated as you annihilate all intruders, won't you?"

He pointed to one of the larger and stronger-looking of the human drones waiting for his command: "You, come with me and protect the entrance to my private quarters. And you, bald human drone"—he pointed at the blank-eyed Mr. Flash—"go downstairs and guard the prisoners. You two," he instructed two other mind-controlled servants—a girl with long, dark hair and her handsome sidekick—"protect the outer doors to my sanctuary. Let no one enter. Kill anyone who tries." He indicated the large double doors at the back of the boardroom, the ones that led to his tower. "The rest of you, assist Nicholas Knox in defending the building."

"What shall I do?" asked Gary in a hesitant squeak.

Nektar pondered this for a moment. It's always difficult to know what to do with the intern in this kind of situation.

"Oh, just . . . just wait by the coffee machine and see if anyone wants one," Nektar decided. And with that, he swept through the double doors with his personal bodyguard and Mr. Flash and slammed them shut behind him. Cowgirl and the Sheriff took up defensive positions outside, their wasp-colored eyes blank and staring.

Nicholas Knox sighed. Once again he was left to do the dirty work.

"Right. Well, all remaining drones, take up positions out there in the hallway. Don't allow anyone to leave the elevators."

The other servants marched woodenly out the door, ignoring Gary's squeak of "Doesn't anyone want a coffee, then?"

Knox followed them but didn't stop in the wide white area off the hallway where the elevators were. On the opposite wall, almost hidden behind some large potted palms, was a small door to which only he had the key.

He walked over and vanished through it, carefully closing and locking it behind him.

At the end of Murph's Minute, Mary and Nellie had been the first into action. Holding tightly to Mary's umbrella, the two of them snuck around to the side of the building, and when they were confident nobody was watching, not even one of the tiny robot wasps they could see zipping around, Mary flew them swiftly up to the roof.

They landed at the exact spot Murph had pointed out to them, the corner where the electrical cables from a nearby power line snaked across to the concrete roof of the factory.

"There should be a box or something up there, where all the power goes into the building," Murph had told them. "When you get there, Nellie needs to try and get a lightning bolt to hit it. That should knock out the power. Then fly back down and we'll all work out how to get inside while it's dark."

Nellie stood at a safe distance from the box, closed her eyes, and concentrated, while Mary looked up and marveled as the cloud directly above them boiled and thickened. Nellie held out her hand, palm upward, gesturing toward the metal box where all the cables disappeared through the roof. She opened her eyes at the crack of thunder.

Just as Knox was saying the word "infiltration" downstairs—which is a word that we've realized sounds weirder the more you say it—a bolt of lightning shot down and hit the box in a shower of sparks.

"Well done, Nellie," marveled Mary.

There was another gigantic thunderclap.

"You can stop it now," Mary said.

"I'm not sure if I can," squeaked Nellie, suddenly looking frightened. **"Watch out!"**

At that moment, another lightning bolt landed right beside them, and Nellie was blown backward. She lay motionless on the rooftop, oblivious to the raindrops falling on her face.

Mary rushed over to her friend. **"Nellie, wake up! Are you okay?"**

But as she knelt down beside her, Mary heard a crackle from behind and noticed a strong smell of burning. Horrified, she looked around and saw a tangled jumble of red-hot metal lying on the wet rooftop. A few seconds ago this metal skeleton with sparks flying from it had been a bright yellow umbrella.

Murph, Billy, and Hilda peeked cautiously out from behind the food truck after the second lightning strike. The huge floodlights that had been illuminating the concrete plaza in front of the Ribbon Robotics factory had gone out, but there was no sign of Mary and Nellie floating back down to join them.

Squinting into the gloom, Murph could just make out the trucks that had been used to attack The School, parked not far from the main factory doors.

Billy's ears inflated, a sure barometer of impending doom. "Murph," he whined, "something's wrong. Where are they?"

"I don't know, Billy," whispered Murph, "but you need to stay calm. We lost Flora and Carl, but they can look after themselves. And the same goes for Mary and Nellie. We'll find them. But whatever's happened, we need to get in there."

Billy's ears deflated slightly.

"Come on, then. This is the part where we spring into action!" Hilda piped up with the enthusiasm of someone who had imagined being on a rescue mission on approximately a daily basis and couldn't quite believe this was happening for real.

The three of them broke cover and ran across the street to the locked gates. Murph noticed a control panel off to one side and realized they were electric.

"The power's out to these things too," he whispered,

pushing the left-hand gate and feeling it move slightly. "Help, quick," he ordered Billy, who got his hand in the gap and began pushing as well.

Over by the building they could see the five guards. Hilda gulped. It was Gangly Fuzz Face and his friends. In his fright, Billy lost control and his hand abruptly swelled to several times its normal size, catapulting the gate open with an ear-shattering *clang*.

"Intruders," intoned Gangly Fuzz Face. "Prepare to attack."

"Over there! Move!" Murph mouthed urgently, and all three of them sprinted the short distance to the first truck and disappeared behind it.

Murph let out a small sigh of relief. Surely they were safe for a moment at least—only someone with X-ray vision would be able to see them there.

"Intruders located behind the vehicle. Prepare to destroy," droned Crazy Eyes Jemima, whose Capability, although nobody has thought to mention it until now, was X-ray vision.

"Understood. Preparing to destroy," answered Corned Beef Boy. They could hear his clumping footsteps as he moved ponderously across the plaza toward them.

A moment later there was a creak and groan as he picked up the entire truck and tossed it to one side as easily as if it had been a small garden gnome.

The Super Zeroes scampered behind another of the trucks with the kind of speed you're only capable of when you're being chased by a brainwashed kid with incredible strength who wants to crush your head like a ripe blueberry.

"Now located behind second vehicle. The intruders appear to be cowering in fear," intoned Jemima.

"Rude," whispered Hilda, although it was largely true.

"Preparing to destroy," replied Corned Beef Boy again, and he began to stomp toward them. **"We're gonna diiiiiiiiiiie,"** whimpered Billy, which was no help at all.

22

Drone War

Nellie groggily opened her eyes and looked around. Smoke was still pouring out of the metal box at the corner of the roof.

"Did we do it?" she asked Mary softly.

Mary nodded, smiling back at her brightly. "There was a slight problem with my umbrella, though." She pointed to the tangle of metal that was still smoking and fizzing beside them. "But never mind. Let's have a look over the edge and see if we can see the others."

Nellie looked serious. "I might not get the chance to say this later, so I want to get it in now," she told Mary. "Whatever happens to us, I just want you to know that I am loving this. Thanks for bringing me along."

"*Bringing you along?* Are you kidding?" replied Mary. "Clouds, thunderbolts . . . you've been the most important person on the whole rescue."

Nellie made a small squeaking noise, because words were not her Capability, and reached out her hand to squeeze Mary affectionately on the foot. But as she made contact there was a sharp spark of static.

"OW!" Mary jerked her foot away. **"You fizzed me!"**

Nellie was looking at her hand in confusion—the one she'd used to call down the lightning. Just visible across her skin were tiny, luminous blue lines of electricity running backward and forward. She'd never really allowed herself to use her power fully before—what was going on?

"What on earth . . . ?" wondered Mary.

But there was no time to stop and think. A huge, grinding crash came from below them—the sort of noise a truck makes when it's picked up and thrown.

"Come on," Mary ordered, holding out her hand to help Nellie to her feet. **"OW! No, the other hand,"** she added a second later.

Nicholas Knox bashed the keys of his computer in frustration. The power outage had knocked out his feed from the spy drones. He was shut in his secret office, completely blind. With a creeping sense of anxiety, Knox began to realize that this could all turn out very badly for him. Nektar had the central matrix for the mind-control helmets on his wrist—the human drones would all follow his orders. The building was under attack and he could only assume that—he shook his head in silent amazement—real superheroes had turned up to rescue the staff and students of The School. And here he was in a room full of evidence showing that he was one of the ringleaders of the whole thing.

There was only one thing to do.

"We're all gonna diiiiiiiiie, all of us," continued Billy, building on his theme slightly.

They were still crouched by one of the enormous wheels of the second truck, peering out from underneath it as the heavy feet of Corned Beef Boy got closer and closer.

As it often did when he was scared or excited, Billy's Capability activated. But this time something was different. Normally it was a hand that ballooned—or his head. But suddenly the huge tire beside him inflated sharply, making the truck lean dangerously to one side. Corned Beef Boy stopped his march to stare at it.

"How on earth did you do that?" asked Murph in a whisper.

"I don't **knoooooooooow**," whimpered Billy.

"Do it again!" Murph said.

"I don't know **hooooooooow**," Billy moaned. He was not one of life's natural copers.

"TRY!" ordered Murph. "Think about what you did. Concentrate on that other tire. Do it! Do it now!"

Billy screwed his face up, thinking of the tire as hard as he could. One of his earlobes puffed up slightly.

"The tire, Billy," urged Murph.

Suddenly, with a rasping and a creaking, the other tire on their side of the truck inflated to several times its normal size, forcing the truck to keel over onto Corned Beef Boy, who only just reached his hands up in time to stop it crushing him.

His four fellow guards watched nervously, not daring to move from their positions in front of the main doors in case this was a diversion.

"Pursue the intruders," Fuzz Face ordered Corned Beef Boy. "Move the vehicle and pursue."

Corned Beef Boy heaved with his shoulders and shoved the truck to one side, where it crashed against the one he'd thrown earlier. The two trashed vehicles were now blocking the main gates.

Murph had led his friends in a crouching run to the other side of truck number three, where he was now doing some extremely quick thinking: "Billy, we know now that you can inflate other things, not just your own body. Right?"

Billy nodded.

"Okay," Murph went on, "listen . . . "

Crazy Eyes Jemima, in her brainwashed mind, was looking forward to telling her master that the three intruders had been destroyed. She watched closely as the silhouette of Corned Beef Boy stomped over to the third truck.

Using her Cape she could discern the outlines of the three targets standing behind the truck, apparently talking urgently to one another. One of them was waving his hands as if explaining something.

She saw her fellow human drone move around the side of the truck and bear down on them, excited that he was about to eliminate his master's enemies. But then something unexpected happened. Corned Beef Boy's head grew enormous. She saw the shape of his mind-control helmet fly into the air as it popped off his suddenly huge head, and then watched as he crumpled to the floor. She rubbed her eyes.

"Our operative has been neutralized," she told Gangly Fuzz Face in blank surprise.

"I will eliminate the intruders," decided Frankenstein's Nephew. He ran toward the enemy at full speed, each of his hands expanding into a ball of flame. He began swinging his arms in a windmill motion in preparation for a devastating attack. But before he could even round

the corner of the truck, his head suddenly ballooned, and then his entire body. Frankenstein's Nephew became a large, partially lit ball. His mind-control helmet flew off and smashed against the factory wall as his momentum carried him onward. He kept on rolling for some distance before hitting the fence and deflating.

Gangly Fuzz Face looked on in astonishment as yet another of his gang was taken out. "I shall inform Lord Nektar we need reinforcements," he said to Crazy Eyes Jemima. "Remain here and prevent the intruders from escaping." He turned on his heel and disappeared inside the building.

Crazy Eyes Jemima turned to her one remaining companion, the boy Murph thought of as Pork Belly Pig Breath, although his name was actually Julian. "We will remain here and prevent the intruders from entering our master's complex."

"No, actually you won't," shouted a voice from far above them.

On the fourth floor, the elevator doors opened with a soft *ting*. Gangly Fuzz Face, mindless servant of the man-wasp

Nektar, was on his way to tell his master that the most powerful member of his gang had been neutralized by intruders.

But there was a problem. The guards, who were also mindless servants of the man-wasp Nektar, had been ordered not to let anyone leave the elevator. And what happened next is a good example of why mind-controlled armies will probably never really catch on.

The large, white, potted-plant-lined room where the elevators were located was being guarded by three human drones—all older students at The School. On one side was the entrance to the corridor that led to the boardroom and Nektar's tower. On the other, as you might remember, was the small, unobtrusive door behind which Nicholas Knox was contemplating the ruin of all his schemes.

Gangly Fuzz Face attempted to step out of the elevator but suddenly found a beefy hand on his chest.

"No one is permitted to leave the elevator," ordered the drone—who before being mind-controlled had been a promising student called Fisher.

"I have a message for Lord Nektar," Gangly Fuzz Face said. "I must be allowed to pass."

"No one is permitted the leave the elevator," explained the second drone, a tall girl who was a goalie for the school hockey team and looked like it.

"I must be allowed to pass. I have a message for Lord Nektar," intoned Gangly Fuzz Face. This is the real problem with brainwashed servants—there's no middle ground.

"Attack the intruder," decided the third drone, which was a real mistake.

"I am a servant of Nektar," said Gangly Fuzz Face. "If you attack me, you are an enemy of Nektar. I will destroy enemies of Nektar."

Well, you can see where this is leading, can't you?

Gangly Fuzz Face attempted to move the third human drone blocking his way using his force-field Capability, slamming him back against one of the potted plants and knocking him unconscious.

The first drone, Fisher, responded to this by attacking Gangly Fuzz Face with his own Capability. This was optimistic, as his Capability was making tiny purple flowers appear out of thin air. Gangly Fuzz Face was blasted in the face by a jet of blossoms, but hit back with another force field that knocked Fisher out as well.

The final guard, the hockey goalie, ran at him and used her own Capability, her rock-hard hands, to smash him backward into the elevator. Unfortunately, she smashed him into the control panel, which meant the doors closed on her, clamping her mind-control helmet between them. She pulled backward instinctively, wrenching the helmet from her head. She too fell to the floor, unconscious.

At that moment the side door opened, and Nicholas Knox cautiously poked his head out. He surveyed the three unconscious students in the room before gingerly peeking into the elevator. Gangly Fuzz Face lay on the floor, snoring loudly underneath the sparking elevator control panel.

Suddenly Knox realized he had no hope of fighting whatever forces were now ranged against him. Who on earth had managed to disable such powerful servants? It was time to abandon his Nektar plan and regroup. His brain was teeming with new ideas, none of which would involve a crazy wasp. He couldn't wait to get started.

He who fights and runs away, thought Knox, *lives to fight another day*. He ducked back through the door to his private office and grabbed a few things, before murmuring to himself: "He who stays and takes a chance, ends up in an ambulance."

Outside the main front doors to Ribbon Robotics, Murph, Billy, and Hilda high-fived each other delightedly.

"Billy, you did it!" enthused Murph.

"I know," replied Billy, grinning so widely it looked like he'd inflated his own mouth. "Did you see me, Hilda? It was amazing! I blew Corned Beef Boy's head up like a, like a . . . like a massive blow-up head. Epic!"

He shouted up to the two silhouetted heads that were peering down from the roof. "Did you see it, Mary? Nice!"

Mary had indeed seen. She and Nellie had rushed to the edge of the roof and looked down, watching with their hearts in their mouths as Corned Beef Boy had stomped around the truck toward their friends. Nellie had just been about to try and summon more lightning when they'd seen Billy flick out his right hand as if throwing a Frisbee and their enemy's head expand with a breathy trumpeting noise. They'd watched as the helmet had been catapulted into the air, landing some distance away on the wet concrete and smashing.

Corned Beef Boy had slumped to the ground, unconscious. And then came Billy's even more impressive dispatch of Frankenstein's Nephew, which had actually made Nellie clap her hands with pride.

Before the remaining two guards had time to react, Mary had swung into action. She had picked up the still-fizzing umbrella skeleton, carefully using her yellow scarf to prevent it from electrocuting her, held it over the edge of the roof, and dropped it. She used the yellow lights of the mind-control helmets to aim precisely at the two figures four floors below.

The effect had been quite dramatic. Their helmets had been short-circuited by the electrified metal, and the two remaining guards were now lying crumpled on the ground, out cold.

Now, mid-celebration, the true implications of this hit Murph. "Mary, was that . . . your umbrella?" he called, suddenly horrified.

"Yes, I'm afraid so. That's why we couldn't fly down from the roof. It sort of got lightning-ed." She laughed a slightly hollow laugh. "No more flying for me—looks like you've got another kid without a Cape on the team."

Murph felt sure Mary must be devastated at the loss of her umbrella. He experienced an odd mixture of pity and pride that she was hiding it so well. "Wait there," he instructed, "we're on our way up." He turned to Billy and Hilda: "Come on, we've got to keep going. We've got them on the run."

They left the darkening plaza and moved into the reception area, which seemed empty and eerie in the yellow emergency lighting. "This way, I think," said Murph, leading them toward the revolving doors.

"Wait a minute. Where do you think you're going?" said a mean voice from away to the right. It was Patsy the receptionist.

"We're, you know, going to the elevators?" said Murph, figuring that sometimes honesty is the best policy.

"What, without signing in?" demanded Patsy angrily. She gestured at a large book on the desk in front of her: **"Nobody goes through without signing in."**

"No, of course," said Murph soothingly. "Er, Hilda, would you sign us in with this nice lady, please?"

Patsy McLean had not been called a nice lady in over seventeen years, and even that time it had been sarcastic. The ghost of a dead smile lingered about her pinched mouth for a fraction of a second as Hilda scribbled their names in the book.

"**Purpose of visit**, it says here." She turned back to Murph. "How do you spell 'thwart'?"

"Just put 'stop,'" suggested Billy.

"Oh yes, right, thanks," said Hilda gratefully.

She stuck out her tongue as she wrote in the **Purpose of visit** column:

Stop evil wasp guy, rescue school, and save day.

"Thank you," said Patsy, handing them laminated

cards with **VISITOR** on them. She really was a terrible receptionist—but of course nobody had ever dared tell her so.

In a flash, the Super Zeroes were off through the revolving doors, which worked far better during a power outage because you could just push them.

"I think the elevator's out of order," shouted Patsy after them. "I heard it exploding or something a minute ago. I'd take the stairs if I were you. On the right."

Murph, Billy, and Hilda sprinted up several flights of stairs and found a fire door right at the top. They opened it by pushing on a bar, and let Mary and Nellie in. There was a brief burst of triumphant dancing as the five Super Zeroes were reunited.

"Right—let's find out what's waiting for us," said Murph, pointing to the door that led into the main building. A sign beside it read: **Fourth Floor—Strictly No Access to Any Personnel without Top Level Security Clearance.** But nobody ever got to be a Hero by taking notice of signs.

There was an electronic pad beside the door where usually you'd need to swipe a security pass—but with the power off, Murph simply gave the door a push and it swung open.

The Super Zeroes found themselves in a white room decorated with potted plants and unconscious teenagers. And just as they entered through one door, someone else came in through another, smaller door off to one side. He was a man with a sharp nose and carefully arranged hair, dressed in a brown coat and carrying a broom.

"Don't attack me. I'm not part of this monster's plans. Please! I'm just a humble cleaner," he explained, brandishing his brush at them.

"What's been going on here?" demanded Murph, pointing to the slumped forms of the guards.

"He took them over with mind-control helmets, that

monster," replied the man, shifting his way around the wall toward the door to the stairs. "Are you part of the rescue mission? Your main strike force must have come through already. What powers do they have?" he asked suddenly, leaning toward them curiously. "Where do their powers come from?"

"Never you mind," interrupted Mary. "Do you know where that wasp guy is now? And where he's holding our friends?"

"From that school?" asked the man dressed as a cleaner. "In his tower, of course. They're all in his tower. Prisoners at the bottom. And you'll find Nektar at the top."

He had finally reached the door to the stairwell, and before anyone could think twice he'd gone through it, shouting, "Make sure you don't let him get away!" over his shoulder as he pounded off down the stairs.

"He had unusually shiny shoes for a member of the domestic staff," Hilda said thoughtfully.

"Leave him. Whoever he is, we don't have time," said Murph. "Get the helmets off these ones." Together, they pried the mind-control helmets from the unconscious

319

guards and, with difficulty, dragged the kids to lie together at one side of the room.

Then all five Super Zeroes crept cautiously into the corridor that led to the glass-walled boardroom and beyond—Nektar's lair.

23

Battle of the Boardroom

Murph looked down the long hallway. Out of the windows to his right he could see the setting sun through the breaking clouds. But with the lights off, the passage was unpleasantly dark. The yellow emergency lighting was still functioning, but it was dim and cast thick black stripes of shadow that could be hiding anything in their depths.

A loud buzzing sound caught his attention. It was a wasp, bashing itself repeatedly against one of the windows. He moved closer to take a look. It was one of the spy drones, but with the power off to Knox's control center, it had nothing to guide it. The drone turned to him, the tiny glass lens of its camera reflecting the faint yellow light, before blundering off down the hall, back the way it had come.

"The entrance to the tower's this way; that's what

the cleaner said," Murph said in a low voice to his friends, "but it'll be guarded. Watch your step."

As they crept down the hallway toward the boardroom, there was a sudden disturbance in the air, as if something had flown past them very fast and left a jet stream in its wake. They looked around but saw nothing.

"Come on," Murph ordered, leading them through into the huge, glass-walled room. Ready for anything, the Super Zeroes spread out in a line and took in their surroundings.

On a large table to one side lay the two remaining attack drones, their guns pointed downward and the lights around their bulging eyes switched off. Wires connected them to an electrical outlet on the wall.

Over at the far end, hard to make out in the dim yellowish lighting, was an untidy pile of tables and chairs: they had been thrown together to form a rough barricade in front of a set of heavy-looking doors.

Murph pointed to the doors, mouthing, *"He must be in there,"* to his friends.

"There's no point in whispering. I can hear you perfectly well."

The five Super Zeroes jumped. The voice had come from behind the barrier of furniture.

"Yes, my master is in there," the voice went on, "but I don't think you're going to be visiting him anytime soon."

"It's Drench," Billy realized. "Super-hearing."

"The official term is Hypersensitive Auditory Capability, and it's 'Mr. Drench' to you. But you can call me 'mighty Nektar's most loyal servant.'"

Where the other human drones had sounded monotonous and zombielike, Mr. Drench was speaking with an excited fervor. Murph shuddered, remembering how disillusioned with his job at The School the teacher had sometimes seemed, how he'd revealed something of his past and his frustration at being thought of as simply a sidekick to Captain Alpha. *What might a mind-control helmet do to the hidden bitterness fermenting away in there*? he wondered.

Murph now caught a glimpse of Mr. Drench's

glasses flashing yellow light back at them from between two piled-up chairs.

"You have done well to come this far," continued Mr. Drench-drone, more resentment bubbling to the surface. "It's clear we underestimated you. Once you have been captured and subdued it will be interesting to interrogate you. You will provide valuable information to help my master crush any future attacks. I am only glad that you have not been able to notify the Heroes' Alliance of the supreme Lord Nektar's plans. By the time they find out it will be too late."

"I imagine he's planning to take over the world or something. They usually are," Mary whispered to Murph.

"Ha!" snapped Mr. Drench. "Yes, we will take over the world. Once my master's loyal servant Knox has created more helmets like mine, we will enroll the whole school in our glorious army." He sounded positively manic by now. **"All will join us in worshipping mighty Nektar, the most powerful. All will join his hive."**

"I think that's bees," started Hilda.

"Silence!" screamed Mr. Drench. **"Seize them!"**

Ever since he had been turned evil by the mind-control helmet, a tiny part of Mr. Drench's brain had really been looking forward to saying, "Seize them!" It's the most fun part about being a bad guy. Just because it felt so good, he said it again, drawing it out for effect: **"Seiiiiiiiiiiiiiiiiize themmmmmmm!"** The Super Zeroes looked around frantically, wondering who he was talking to.

"Quick, back into the hallway," decided Murph,

but when they turned around, they found the doorway behind them was blocked. Dirk Scott stood there, his black-and-yellow eyes fixed on them.

Murph remembered the blast of air they'd felt out in the passageway. The Sheriff had used his Capability to flash past them and cut off their way back.

"You will not escape," said Dirk in a droning voice. "We will control you."

"Not today!" sang Nellie, diving toward him with her hand outstretched.

Dirk was too startled and too brainwashed to get out of the way. Nellie's hand connected with his face, hitting him with a jolt of lightning-bolt electricity. He jerked and smashed back against the door, sparks flying from his yellow helmet as the lights along the sides of it went out. Dirk slumped to the floor.

"Well, that's new," marveled Murph. "When did you figure out you could do that?"

"About five seconds ago," replied Nellie shyly. They grinned at each other, and everything seemed great for about seventeen twenty-fourths of two seconds.

"Seize them!" shrieked Mr. Drench,

who was incredibly excited to get this line for a third time and really gave it everything he'd got.

With horror, the Super Zeroes saw the dark silhouette of Deborah Lamington move out from behind the barricade of tables and chairs. And Cowgirl was spinning a rope lasso. The yellow strip of lights along the side of her head flashed as she spun the rope faster and faster. The heavy form of Dirk was blocking the doors behind them—there was no way out.

"You will be captured and subjugated. There is no escape. You will join us as loyal servants of Nektar," explained Cowgirl unhelpfully.

But before she could launch her lasso, there was a huge clang that sounded like the back of somebody's head being hit with a frying pan. There was an excellent reason it sounded like that. Behind her was a lanky teenage boy holding a large frying pan. Deborah fell forward, stunned, and Hilda raced across and snatched the helmet from her head before she had a chance to come around.

"Where did you spring from?" asked Mary.

"Over there by the coffee machine," squeaked the teenager. "Nektar told me to wait there, so I did. Anyway, my name's Gary—and I think my internship placement here just ended."

"Why do you have a large frying pan?" Billy wanted to know, but there was no time for Gary to answer.

"You will never defeat Nektar!"

came a weaselly voice from the back of the room. Mr. Drench was standing in front of the barricade that guarded the double doors to Nektar's tower. "You are not Alliance operatives. You are not Heroes. You have no potential," he spat.

But then he took another look.

In front of him stood the boy who had started the school year with no Capability, no friends, and no confidence. But now Murph's eyes were narrowed, his feet planted firmly apart in determination. To his right, Mary

tightened the belt on her yellow raincoat in preparation for battle. Beside her, Hilda tossed her hair and snorted like a thoroughbred racehorse; she felt she needed a cool move for this dramatic moment and that was all she could think of. To Murph's left stood Nellie, her eyes bright behind her straggly dark hair, her fists clenched. And beside her stood Billy, his head high with confidence and his gaze steady.

They were a team, and they were not going to give in.

Their leader nodded toward Mr. Drench. **"Pop him, Billy,"** said Kid Normal.

It was never going to become one of the classic catchphrases, but Balloon Boy knew what to do. He flicked out his hand, and Mr. Drench's head suddenly expanded—his feathery hair standing on end and his eyes bulging like huge bloodshot marbles. His mind-control helmet flew into the air and shattered against the ceiling. He slumped to the floor, and his head rapidly deflated with a noise like a badly behaved toddler at a posh opera.

For a moment, the Super Zeroes stood in silence,

contemplating how far they'd come. Then they contemplated how far they still had to go, which was less inspiring. Mary broke the silence.

"Tower?"

"Tower," confirmed Kid Normal.

"I'm just gonna go if that's okay?" said Gary softly, tiptoeing toward the exit.

24

Nektar's Nemesis

When Arabella Ribbon bought the factory to set up her robotics business many years ago, she wondered why there was a large tower rising from one side of it. The real estate agent who sold it to her claimed that it was because it had previously been a factory that tested elevators, but real estate agents tend to lie a lot. Anyway, a tower there was—a tall, round tower on the southern end of the building, only accessible by the single set of double doors through which the Super Zeroes now crept.

A year ago it had housed nothing much except Arabella's large, round office, which was right at the top, because she liked to look out at the view and work out how much of it she could buy. Underneath that was a series of storerooms, and, at the very bottom, below ground level, was a large, round empty area which, if the real estate agent was telling the truth, was where the elevators would plummet into if the testing didn't go well.

But that was many months ago. Since then, the tower had become the private domain of Nektar, hideous genetic freakazoid that he was. And things had changed.

If you've never seen a wasp's nest, here's a quick summary. A load of wasps who get along well decide to set up home together. So they chew stuff up, then stick it together with their own spit to make an elaborate nest for themselves, usually in the attic of someone's house.

Now take what we just told you about wasps and imagine a person doing the same thing. In other words, it really was truly one of the grossest things the Super Zeroes had ever seen in their entire lives. Now brace yourself and let's have a look, shall we?

The cardboard, paper, wood, cables, and metal that had been stored in the rooms on the tower's lower floors had been smashed, mashed, and, in some cases, chewed together. They'd then been plastered with—yes—Nektar's own sticky mouth juices to line the walls and ceilings.

So the rooms and hallways of Nektar's tower didn't look like normal rooms and hallways, with nice clean lines and corners where walls, floors, and ceilings met each other. Instead, they were rounded, like the insides of an intestine or a really expensive film set. It was like walking into another planet.

And it really, really stank. You know how bad it smells when relatives—grandmas are the worst offenders—do that thing where they lick their fingers and use them to clean your face? Well, take that smell of stale lick and multiply it by a thousand. Then add ten. That's kind of what it smelled like inside the tower that had become Nektar's lair.

Remember, he'd been in there sticking stuff together with his spit for the best part of a year. And we don't know about you, but we certainly don't remember him taking a toothbrush with him.

The rounded passageways of the nest were dark and creepy-looking. As Murph and the rest of the Super Zeroes stood in the first chamber, they could see two main routes open to them. One curved upward; the other down. Once they had been staircases, but now, coated with crispy mush, they looked more like tubes.

"Don't for goodness' sake say we have to split up," said Hilda.

Murph had, in fact, been about to use those exact words. "Why not?" he asked.

"Nothing good ever happens when people split up. Have you never watched a movie, like, ever?" Hilda said, turning to him and putting her hands on her hips. "It's like in a creepy TV show when someone goes into a dark house but doesn't just turn all the lights on. The rules should be simple: Don't split up. Turn the lights on. When you split up or stumble around in the dark, something awful always happens."

Nellie nodded sagely; she was quite a fan of horror films, and this sounded like good advice.

"Well, there were some lights on in the rest of the factory," reasoned Murph, "so we should be able to sort the lights out at least. Must be an emergency system." He turned back to the doors and scanned the walls on either side for light switches. He spotted them—almost hidden underneath layers of mashed-up and stuck-together goo.

Clenching his teeth, Murph pushed his hand through the covering, which was dry and papery thin, and flicked all the switches down.

There was a flicking, blinking noise as a few lights came on through the tower. But because they were hidden underneath layers of pulpy, stinking nest material, they only cast a pale, brownish light that made the way forward look even creepier, if anything.

"Okay," said Murph, trying to sound more confident than he felt, "the lights are on." He paused. "But we are going to have to split up, just for a bit. Hilda, Billy, you head down and see if you can locate where the rest of The School are being held. Mary, Nellie, you come with me. Let's see if we can find out where wasp guy is hanging out."

All five looked at one another for a long moment. This was it. Then they separated and headed off along the gloomy, sloping, stinking passageways.

Here and there, patches of the real staircases beneath were visible, and Murph tried to walk on them wherever he could. But sometimes it was impossible to avoid stepping on the crushed debris that covered almost every surface. It made a papery crunching sound every time he moved; it was impossible to creep along silently. Whatever was waiting for them at the top of the tower would have plenty of warning that they were coming.

Hilda and Billy crept down the other passageway—which was built around a spiral staircase that seemed to wind its way toward the base of the tower. As they neared the bottom they could hear whistling, and as they peered around the final curve they could make out a large figure pacing backward and forward.

It was Mr. Flash. Behind him they could see that a huge, thick metal wall had been constructed across the middle of the large room at the bottom of the tower, with a door fashioned from iron bars in the center. One of the bars was frosted with ice—clearly someone had tried to use their Capability to escape but with no success. Another of the bars seemed to be splattered with soup.

"That must be where they're keeping everyone," whispered Hilda as they cowered at the corner of the corridor. "Okay," she went on, thinking fast. "So all we need to do is get past Mr. Flash, then get that door open."

Just contemplating this made her let out a small whimper of fear. And not out of her mouth either. But this was no time to hesitate. She grabbed Billy's arm: "Come on, let's get in there and pop him!"

Mr. Flash saw them as soon as they rounded the corner. In his brainwashed state, he continued to believe that his primary function was to serve Nektar, and as with Mr. Drench, the mind-control helmet had also apparently amplified his nastier side. **_WHAT THE PURPLE SPROUTING BROCCOLI ARE YOU TWO DOING HERE?_** he roared at them. **_I WAS EXPECTING A GENUINE RESCUE MISSION, NOT A PAIR OF LAME GEESE._**

"Good evening, Mr. Flash," replied Hilda, who had been taught that good manners should never be forgotten. "Your eyes look, er, very striking."

"Shut up, horse girl, and get in the cage with the rest of them," ordered the teacher.

"I don't think so, Mr. Flash," began Billy politely, summoning up his head-popping Capability. But Mr. Flash was ready for him. He seemed to vanish, appearing suddenly behind them and bellowing so loudly that Billy inflated his own nose in shock. They spun to face the teacher, but he moved again, so fast that it was impossible to keep track of where he was.

"Billy . . . ?" Hilda said nervously out of the corner of her mouth.

"I . . . I can't," wailed Billy. "He's too fast for me to get a fix on him!"

Mr. Flash appeared on the far side of the room, roared with laughter, and produced a set of keys, which he dangled from one meaty finger. "Did you really think you were going to defeat me, get these keys, and rescue these folks?" he shouted like a sarcastic steam train. "Some have tried to escape already. I had to have a word with a couple of them." He gestured toward the bars, behind which they could just make out a prone figure lying on the hard floor. "Knocked out cold," Flash gloated, "just like your precious Mr. Souperman."

Suddenly he flung the keys to one side. "Come on, then," he goaded them, as the keys tinkled on the concrete floor. "Let's see what Fat Finger Boy and Little Horsey Girl can do, shall we?"

Before they could react, he was right in front of them, hopping from foot to foot and smashing his fists together. "I will overpower you for the glory of Nektar," he gloated.

"Keep him talking," whispered Hilda, as she concentrated hard.

"What about?" hissed Billy.

"Anything!" she said urgently. "Sports, cheese, marsupials . . ."

"What's your favorite bird of prey?" screeched Billy in a panic.

"What?" Mr. Flash stopped hopping and looked at him furiously.

"Mine's an eagle," said Billy eagerly, and proceeded to do his best impression of one: **"Ka-kaaark!"**

"That's nothing like an eagle, idiotic boy," snapped Mr. Flash, forgetting what he was supposed to be doing for a moment. He didn't notice the whinnying sound as, away to his right, two tiny horses appeared out of nowhere. "An eagle's much higher-pitched than that."

"What, more like **ka-keeeeeek!**" suggested Billy, covering up the faint clinking sound as the first horse picked up the keys in its miniature teeth and cantered toward the bars.

"No! It's more like a screech," began Mr. Flash, but then he remembered he was supposed to be destroying his master's enemies, not discussing birdcalls. "Anyway, shut up. It's time to finish you off. Like you ever stood a chance against me— two kids against the mighty Mr. Flash!"

"Actually, Iain," said Hilda, "I think you'll find our odds have improved." She flicked her head toward the cage behind him.

Flash turned just in time to see the doors swing open and the students and teachers of The School file out, each and every one looking directly at the man who had imprisoned them, with an expression that said, "You're about to pay for that."

"Bit of a rookie mistake, the old 'fling the keys away' move, wouldn't you say?" continued Hilda.

There was a moment of tense silence as Mr. Flash contemplated his situation. It was Billy who broke the deadlock. **"Charge?"** he suggested politely, inflating himself to block the entrance to the staircase.

High above them, Murph, Mary, and Nellie continued up the spiral passageway to Nektar's lair. Murph wondered what they were about to face.

Mary and Nellie had seen Nektar when he attacked The School, but all Murph had to go on was their description. Crazy images flashed through his mind as the papery floor crackled under his feet. A wasp that could talk? A man who could fly? A normal wasp, but two yards long? An inch-long man-head with a wasp's body?

Regardless of what Nektar was, Murph told himself, he was dangerous and had managed to do some serious damage to their school, teachers, and fellow students. They'd come too far to give up now, no matter how scared they were.

At the final corner before the top of the tower, the passageway was blocked by the huge silhouette of a guard—the figure was lit from behind and cast a giant shadow. It was clear that Nektar had chosen the most beefy, the most enormous, the most impressive specimen he could to protect his inner sanctum. Murph, Mary, and Nellie froze on the spot.

"Who are the intruders?" they heard a peevish voice cry out in the distance. The huge silhouette moved slightly as the guard peered in their direction.

"They are no one to fear, Lord Nektar," belched a

deep voice. "It's a lame kid called Murph and two of his friends. I shall eliminate them."

"Well, hurry up—PICNIC!" they heard the faint voice shout. The giant figure started to move down the passageway toward them, the crispy covering clicking and cracking under his enormous feet.

"Uh-oh," whispered Murph. "Now what do we do? And who on earth *is* that?"

"Stay calm," said Mary. "Let me do the talking." She raised her voice and spoke in a calm tone, as if trying to soothe an anxious cow: "Hello! You seem like a reasonable guy. I want to make a deal with you. How about—"

But there was to be no deal. The guard strained his huge muscles and cried out: "Defend Lord Nektar! Activating Capability!"

Murph and his friends waited, terrified. What Capability could this beast have, to have been chosen as Nektar's final guard? Super-strength? Breathing fire? Spitting out rocks?

Murph could just make out that the figure was opening his mouth, baring two rows of very large white teeth. All at once, there was a piercing, screeching noise.

"It's Barry Talbot!" Mary cried. "The boy who can make a screeching noise with his teeth!"

"Worst. Cape. Ever," said Murph grimly, sticking his fingers in his ears.

Suddenly there was a flash and a bang. Barry flew off his enormous feet, hit the wall behind him, and slumped in a heap on the floor. He was out cold.

Mary and Murph turned around to see a very sheepish Nellie with a startled expression on her face.

"Nellie!" exclaimed Murph, but then ran out of conventional words and just added **"Mahumbah?"**

"Um, sorry, it just sort of happened," squeaked Nellie. "That noise was really, really annoying. And besides, I'm sick of people treating us like useless ants. Plus, we haven't got time to mess around; we have a school to save." It was the longest speech she'd ever made by a factor of . . . well, a lot. She put her hands on her hips in the internationally recognized Hero pose.

"Wow, you go, girl!" said Murph.

"Don't ever say that again," Mary warned him. "You can't pull it off."

The three of them stepped over the giant snoozing form of Barry Talbot, kicking the final mind-control helmet from his head as they went, and approached Nektar's command center.

Their feet were still sticking to the tacky, lick-infused floor, and as they climbed the final part of the staircase, they started to hear crackly, distant music. It sounded scratchy and old-fashioned and, frankly, unnerving.

At the top of the tower, a set of wooden double doors stood slightly ajar. The team pushed them open slowly and surveyed the round, window-lined room at the top. It was lit with yellowish sunset light. The walls were plastered with Nektar's nesting materials, and they could see a few wooden cupboards and cabinets stuck in among the goo. An old-fashioned record player was the source of the creepy music.

And right in the middle, sitting in a chair with his back to them, was the wasp himself.

Nektar was softly singing along with the reedy voice on the old record:

"Free, free, free, and busy as a bee.
Oh, I mustn't grumble, always be humble,

That makes me a bumble,
I'm free, free, free, and busy as a bee."

It sounded awful—out of tune and croaky. If you want details—just imagine what it would be like if a wasp started singing at you.

The man-wasp interrupted his own singing: "Hello, little pests." He continued with the universally approved bad guy opening remark: "I've been expecting you. Did you like my song?"

"Um, not really," said Murph honestly. "It was quite disturbing."

In fact, the music had just become even more odd. The record had stuck and kept repeating the same line over and over again:

Free, free, free, and busy as a bee.

"Why are you listening to a song about bees when you're a wasp?" Mary wanted to know.

Nektar lurched to his feet and advanced toward them in total fury. "Why doesn't everybody just SHUT UP ABOUT BEES! Bees, bees, bees. Oh, we're so cute and bumbly. Look at us sipping the pollen from the pretty flowers! Look at our fuzzy little backs! I'm sick to death of bees! Why does everyone think bees are so great, eh? ANSWER ME!"

Free, free, free, and busy as a bee.

By now he was looming over them, eyes bulging, spit flying from his mouth, fists clenched, and venom dripping from the stingers on his wrists. It was quite terrifying. For just a second, Murph felt he had seen inside the mind of a wasp—a lonely, mean bully who doesn't understand why everybody prefers bees.

"Honey?" he suggested rather lamely.

"Honey?" roared Nektar, turning away from them and kicking the record player over, which was something of a relief. "I'll give you some honey." This made no sense, but his next sentence clarified things somewhat: "I am Nektar and you are about to become extinct, and your stupid friends and your stupid school are all going to bow down to KING NEKTAR! The king . . . bee . . ."

"Queen bee?" suggested Mary, at exactly the same time Murph suggested, "King wasp?"

"SHUT UP!" roared Nektar, glaring at them with total hatred. *"This is where your little rescue mission ends. In DEATH!"*

And he charged at them, flailing his stingers around wildly. The Super Zeroes scattered—Mary diving between his legs, Murph throwing himself to one side. As Nektar lunged to try to intercept him, Nellie saw her moment. She jumped as high as she could and swung her hand at his face, hoping with all her might that she had some electrical charge left from her lightning bolt.

She didn't.

Nellie's open palm landed on the side of Nektar's pale face with a sharp smacking sound. Her momentum carried her on past him, within inches of one of his dripping stingers, but she managed to roll as she landed, coming up beside Murph and Mary, who were now regrouping off to one side, panting and looking worried. She looked down at her hands, but the tiny blue lines of electricity had disappeared. She was out of charge. A giant man-wasp had charged at them, and basically she had just slapped him across the face.

Murph, Nellie, and Mary all felt the same feeling at the very same time. They had made it this far, but if they were being honest with themselves, they hadn't expected it to go quite so well. Now, at the end, they were out of powers and temporarily out of ideas.

The slap seemed to have startled Nektar, but he quickly composed himself. He swung around to face his three enemies, apparently noticing their worried expressions.

"There's no stopping me now," he cackled. "I control the minds of your most powerful friends. And you know what that means, don't you?" He lifted the control unit on his wrist to his mouth. *"Human drones! Protect Lord Nektar! Come to me! Destroy the intruders!"*

In preparation for watching his final victory, he backed away toward the open doors to the balcony. The wind was blowing and the sky moody.

But the human drones did not come.

"Give it up, Nektar," said Murph, rallying slightly. "You're done. There's no one left to help you now. We've taken out your mind-controlled servants—you're on your own."

Nektar frantically pressed the buttons on the black watch, muttering, *"Human drones! Protect your master! Knox! Do you read me?"* but after a moment he seemed to realize there was no point. Angrily, he ripped the box from his wrist and threw it away. It skittered across the floor past Mary's feet and came to rest against the wall. Nektar raised his head, looking straight at Murph with a rather unnerving expression.

"You always were a courageous little fighter," he crooned, ramping up his creepiness by several notches.

Murph looked puzzled. Glancing around at Nellie and Mary, he responded in the only way possible to this new development.

"Huh?"

"Yes—even as a baby," continued Nektar.

"I'm sorry, I don't . . . Hang on, what on earth are you talking about?" Murph demanded.

"Oh . . . you don't know?" said Nektar.

"Know what?" replied Murph cautiously.

Nektar looked at him fondly. "Murph, I am your father."

There was a pause. A long pause. Nellie and Mary froze in horror.

"No, you're not," said Murph disgustedly. "My dad moved to Bristol with his new girlfriend years ago. I see him most holidays. Plus, you're a wasp and my mom wouldn't be seen dead with you." All three of them laughed.

"Well, it was worth a try," said Nektar.

"Not really," Murph replied. "You're even crazier than we thought."

"Don't be so mean to your old daddy!" said Nektar, stung by this.

"We've literally just gone over this. You're not my dad!" Murph reminded him. "You're a crazed wasp-based villain and we're about to finish your reign of terror."

"I don't think so," threatened Nektar. "All this messing around is futile because you're about to become kid soup." He laughed maniacally and grabbed the remote-control unit clamped to his belt. He pressed the single yellow button in the center: *"Attack drones, stand by!"*

The lights dimmed, and Murph heard a horribly familiar humming sound.

There was a smashing noise from below as the two remaining attack drones roared into life down in the boardroom. They disconnected from their electrical outlets, crashed through the windows, and within seconds rose up behind Lord Nektar, flanking him on

either side, looking angry and fiery and ready to take out the Zeroes. "Say hello to my little friends," gloated the man-wasp. "And wave goodbye to your lives."

All three of them gulped. There was nowhere to hide, no time to run.

Nektar twisted his face into an ugly, smug grin, confident he had the upper hand. But suddenly there was a shout from outside the half-open doors: **"Stop right there, you waspy loon!"**

The door was kicked open to reveal Hilda framed in the passageway. She had her arms stretched out in front of her—and Nektar's already massive eyes widened even further as her two horses neighed into being and made a beeline—or possibly wasp-line—toward him. Momentarily freaked out, Nektar backed away, out onto his balcony. But then he composed himself.

"Miniature horses? What on earth do you think you're going to do with those stupid things?"

Hilda's eyes darkened. If there was one thing she couldn't bear, it was anyone insulting her horses. All three of them tossed their manes angrily.

"Well, I'd rather be a small horse than a big wasp," taunted Hilda furiously. "And besides, you look like a stupid wasp anyway. You've got the big eyes and the bad attitude, but you don't even have the one useful thing wasps have!"

"Oh yes," said Nektar, preparing to wipe out these infuriating little insects. "And what might that be?"

"Wings!" cried Hilda. **"Pop 'em, Billy!"**

Billy appeared at her shoulder, and with a confident flicking motion, he gestured toward the horses. There was a sound like a neigh mixed with the noise of a balloon inflating as the horses enlarged into two huge, powerful stallions. They reared on their hind legs in front of the terrified Nektar.

Murph, Mary, and Nellie had taken shelter behind what turned out to be Nektar's jam cabinet.

"Who has a jam cabinet?" asked Nellie scathingly.

"At this point, I'm afraid to say that the jam cabinet is one of the least weird things about this guy," Mary replied.

Nellie nodded in agreement. "Fair point."

Nektar was cowering at the very edge of the balcony as the horses reared in front of him. "No! Stay back! Good horsey! Want a carrot?"

Nektar didn't have any carrots. And, quite frankly, it wouldn't have mattered if he did. Because he was very quickly on the receiving end of an almighty hoof in the chest—which sent him teetering dangerously, flailing his arms in circles as he tried to keep his balance.

But as he was about to fall, his waspish brain concocted one last evil thought. Grasping his remote control, he pressed the button and screamed, "Attack drones!

KILL THE SUPER ZEROES!" just as Hilda's

second horse lashed out with a white hoof and punted him over the edge like a novelty wasp-shaped football.

As he fell, the remote control flew out of his hand and seemed to hang in the air for a moment.

Murph had already seen his opportunity. He was lunging for the edge of the balcony as fast as he could, only dimly aware of a *click* as the attack drones readied their machine guns to fire on his friends.

As the sun sent a few last red beams through the low cloud, Kid Normal leaped out into the sunset. He caught the remote control in midair, pressed the yellow button, and just had time to gasp, **"Drones disengage!"** before he plummeted toward the concrete far below.

25

The Heroes' Vow

"That," said the tall, thin woman sitting in Mr. Souperman's office, "is one of the single bravest things I have ever seen."

She clicked a remote control, and on a large screen on the wall a video feed from the attack drone's onboard camera froze at the very moment Murph was about to plummet toward the ground. His face was set, his teeth gritted with total determination to save his friends.

"Brave?" grunted Mr. Flash, now free of his mind-control helmet and feeling much better after spending a few hours unconscious. "Stupid, more like it. This is what happens when civilians get involved. Never ends well."

"I wonder what was going through his head," murmured Mr. Souperman.

Nobody spoke for a moment.

The tall, thin woman broke the silence. "Well," she said, "why don't we ask him?"

What had been going through Murph's head was more like a noise than any particular words, and it's very difficult to write down. But it kind of sounds like the roar of a bear in slow motion and it is, as the tall lady had correctly identified, the sound of bravery. You might think something very noble goes through your mind as you do an extremely fearless thing, but actually it's a noise more like **Bwooooooaaaaa aaaaaarrrrrrrrggggggggghhh hhhhhhhh.**

Told you it was hard to write down.

Anyway—that was what was roaring through Kid Normal's head as he threw himself from Nektar's balcony and learned, just for a split second, what it felt like to fly. Then he learned what it's like to fall rapidly toward the ground, which is a much less fun lesson. One that would have ended with a splatting sound approximately seven seconds later if Murph hadn't had a good friend standing by.

As soon as she had heard Murph gasp, "Drones disengage," Mary had started sprinting toward him. She too had dived into nothingness with that slowed-down bear noise roaring in her own head as she tilted her body like a skydiver, desperately chasing the plunging figure.

She hadn't stopped to think, "I don't have my umbrella." She hadn't even remembered Mr. Flash's scornful words about her Cape. She just knew that she had to save her best friend.

Inches from the ground, Mary managed to grab one of Murph's frantically windmilling hands and suddenly, miraculously, without even thinking about her umbrella, the friends swooped back into the air.

They had
been so close to
disaster that one of
Murph's sneakers
actually brushed the
concrete as she hoisted
him upward, away from a
messy end.

When they'd bobbed
back up above the balcony,
they'd found their three
friends watching open-
mouthed, little Hilda actually
hopping up and down with
excitement and fright.

"What about the
umbrella, then?"

gasped Murph as they landed neatly back on top of the tower.

"Looks like I didn't need it after all," said Mary shakily. "Maybe it just helps to be holding onto something that makes me happy." She looked down at her hand, which was still gripping tightly to Murph's.

Murph immediately exhibited the biggest blush ever recorded, one of those ones that makes you feel like your ears are actually on fire.

To cover his confusion, he looked down over the edge of the balcony, and it was only then that he realized what he'd seen on the ground below them. Or rather— what he hadn't seen. He hadn't seen the squished remains of a man-wasp creature. What had happened to Nektar? As he surveyed the scene down there, his confusion grew.

Several plain black vans had drawn up in the front courtyard of Ribbon Robotics, and a selection of rather tough-looking men and women in black combat gear were moving around purposefully. Murph made out a flash of yellow in the back of one of the vehicles before someone in black slammed the doors shut and banged sharply on the side.

The engine roared as the van sped away through the gates, passing the smashed remains of the Ribbon Robotics trucks they had hidden behind during their battle with Corned Beef Boy. The trucks had been neatly moved to one side, but Murph couldn't for the life of him think how.

"Who on earth are these guys?" he wondered out loud.

"Most of you folks just call us the Cleaners," said a deep voice behind him. Murph turned to see a huge man in black army fatigues and a chunky and almost certainly bulletproof vest. He had short, clipped hair and a face that looked like it wouldn't smile if you tickled it for seven entire years. He was turning over one of the deactivated attack drones with a large, scuffed black boot.

"Cleaners?" said Billy, who was staring at him with his mouth open.

"Cleaners," confirmed the man without looking at him, "because we clean up the mess you lot leave behind. Sort out the likes of them." He pointed to the road beyond the gates, where a TV news van was pulling up beside several police cars that were blocking off the road. "You'll be amazed how easy they can be to fool," the serious man went on, examining the huge drone curiously. "Gas explosion, we usually tell 'em for this kind of thing. Anyway—time to make yourselves scarce. We'll get you home."

That reminded Murph. "Oh yeah, my home. It kind of got destroyed."

"There's been a team there for the last hour," the man told him. "We've got your mom and brother safe. We cooked up a story for them as well."

"What did you tell them?" Murph wanted to know.

"Gas explosion," said the man, without cracking a smile. "Right, come on downstairs with me. I'll let CAMU take you from here," he added, pointing to the police cars.

"CAMU?" said Murph. He'd heard Deborah Lamington use that word when she was talking to the police that night she'd floored a mugger with a trash-can lid. It seemed like years ago.

"Capability Awareness and Management Unit," the man explained. "They're the part of the police that keeps an eye out for this kind of threat and passes the information on to the Heroes' Alliance. They let this wasp guy slip through the net, though. Lucky you were quick on your feet."

Murph felt his head swelling with pride. "Um, thanks." His battle-addled brain slowly clanked into life. "So, wait—the Alliance helps out by providing Heroes when they're needed, and you're here to keep anyone from finding out about it all?"

"We're here to clear up if something goes wrong," the huge man corrected him. "You're not really supposed to leave destroyed factories and trashed houses behind you. It makes us rather unhappy."

"Well, thanks for stepping in," said Murph awkwardly. "See you around, I guess."

The man regarded him coolly with his steely-gray eyes. "I very much hope not, Mr. Cooper."

And so Murph had been driven to a hotel by someone who looked very much like an ordinary police officer, although he now knew she was a member of the Capability Awareness and Management Unit. When Murph arrived, he had listened to his mom explain tearfully that there had been a gas explosion at their house.

I know a lot of secrets all of a sudden, thought Kid Normal to himself, tucked up under tight sheets in an unfamiliar bed.

And when he left for school the following day, with his mom reassuring him that the insurance company had promised to sort everything out, he realized he finally understood what part of the Heroes' Vow meant—the part that talked about secrets. Because he and his friends had just rescued their entire school—and yet there was nobody they could tell.

The rest of The School had similar secrets to deal with. They'd been rounded up at Ribbon Robotics by the mysterious people known as Cleaners and checked over by a very efficient team of doctors. Arriving back at school in blacked-out vans, they'd discovered that the parents who'd arrived to collect them had been told there was a dangerous gas leak and the street had been cordoned off. The hidden machinery of the Capable world had swung into action with breath-taking efficiency. The whole attack, the kidnapping, the battle . . . it was all being expertly covered up.

The students who'd been mind-controlled were

unable to remember anything about the experience when they regained consciousness. The others were warned by the Cleaners, as they sent them on their way, that the entire incident was now classified. Even their parents weren't to be told.

Back in Mr. Souperman's office, the tall, thin lady turned away from the frozen image of Murph leaping into space.

"Saving without glory. Fighting without fear," she said to Mr. Souperman. "They seem to be likely candidates."

Mr. Flash had just been taking a sip of tea and spluttered so hard at this that it came fountaining out of his nose and soaked his mustache. "You're not thinking of taking that bunch of chancers on for the Alliance?" he finally managed to say. **_YOU'RE OFF YOUR ROCKER!_**

"I am the head of the Heroes' Alliance," said the woman calmly, taking a delicate sip of her own tea and getting it nowhere near her nostrils, "and I beg to differ."

"But one of them hasn't even got a Capability!" thundered Mr. Flash. **_YOU CAN'T BE A_**

SUPERHERO WITHOUT SUPER-POWERS.'

"Actually, I think young Mr. Cooper has just proved that you can," said a voice from the doorway.

They all spun around to see Flora appear, looking a bit battered but very much alive. Carl was in the hallway behind her, beating dust out of his pants with a rolled-up newspaper.

Flora walked calmly into the room and sat down. "Sorry for the delay. Crashed jet cars are a real pain to cover up. It's taken us all night to get back here. I don't think we've been introduced," she added, turning to the tall, thin lady.

"I'm Flint—Miss Flint, chief officer of the Heroes' Alliance," she said, extending a hand.

"Blue Phantom," replied Flora, taking the hand and shaking it enthusiastically, "founding member of the Heroes' Alliance. Pleased to meet you."

Miss Flint seemed lost for words at suddenly being confronted with someone who she thought was probably fictional and definitely no longer alive. But she soon composed herself.

"We were just discussing their performance at the factory," she told Flora, pointing to the screen. "I understand it was you and your husband who flew them there."

Flora was silent for a moment, sitting down slowly at the table with her head bowed. Then, suddenly, a single tear fell onto the polished wood. "We did fly them there, yes. We were on our way to mount a rescue, and I thought they'd be safer if I brought them along," she said in a choked voice. "But I let them down. I left them unprotected. I swore I'd never, ever let that happen again."

Carl, who'd walked up behind her, gave her a comforting squeeze on the shoulder. "We came under attack, love. That wasp had more firepower than we thought. It wasn't your fault."

This all seemed to help Miss Flint make up her mind. "So, they were left alone at the start of a mission and still managed to fight their way through. What did you say this team call themselves, Geoffrey?" she asked, turning to Mr. Souperman.

"The, ah, Super Zeroes," he replied. "I think it started

as a bit of a joke among the other children. But they seemed to, you know . . ."

"Turn their weakness into a strength?" Miss Flint finished for him, nodding approvingly. "I'm impressed. Yes, I think we can expect great things from the Super Zeroes."

Later that day, the whole school assembled in the auditorium. All except for Mr. Drench, who hadn't been seen since the battle at Ribbon Robotics. But the rest of the kids and staff had all filed in, intrigued by a message from Mr. Souperman telling them that a rare event was about to take place.

They gathered in the auditorium, still chattering excitedly about the events of the previous day.

Once The School was assembled, the head got to his feet.

For a former Hero, he could get surprisingly tongue-tied speaking in front of large crowds, and he even managed to screw up his rather simple opening line. "Please be sitted," he told the room, before correcting himself but getting it wrong again: "Please be sat."

He coughed to cover his embarrassment, but the scraping of more than a hundred people sitting down on their seats gave him time to collect himself.

"We are in the presence of a very special guest today," he told The School. "Please welcome the head of the Heroes' Alliance."

There was a gasp as Miss Flint stepped forward, gesturing with her hands to keep everyone sitting down.

"Please don't get up," she told them. "And it's nice to see you. I'd never had the pleasure of visiting until we welcomed two of you into the Alliance last year." She nodded toward the back of the room, where Deborah and Dirk were sitting, looking rather downhearted that yesterday they had been the ones who'd needed rescuing.

"We don't admit many people," continued Miss Flint, "but I'm sure you will agree that the five who saved each and every one of you yesterday have proven themselves to be a very impressive team indeed. Would you join me up here, please?"

She beckoned to Murph, Mary, Nellie, Hilda, and

Billy, who were seated in the front row. Looking rather shell-shocked, they shuffled up onto the stage, cheeks burning, and stood in an awkward line directly beneath the stone tablet with the Heroes' Vow carved on it.

"When we admit you to our alliance, we ask you to choose a name that you will adopt while you are on operations," Miss Flint said solemnly. "Name yourselves."

She gestured to Mary, who stepped forward and cleared her throat.

"Mary Canary," she said confidently. Someone tittered.

Hilda stepped forward.

"Equana," she declared.

Next was Billy.

"Balloon Boy," he said boldly.

Nellie was next, and her hair was covering her face as usual. But all at once she brushed it back and looked confidently at the packed room as she stated her chosen name:

"Rain Shadow."

Murph was last. He planted his feet firmly at the edge of the stage as he told the whole assembled school his new name. The name that had started as an insult but that he had made his own.

"I am Kid Normal," said Murph Cooper, "and together we are the Super Zeroes."

Miss Flint nodded calmly. "Take your vow," she instructed them. And together the Super Zeroes recited aloud the words carved into the stone:

I promise to save without glory,
To help without thanks,
And to fight without fear.
I promise to keep our secrets,
Uphold our vow,
And learn what it means
To be a true Hero.

Miss Flint began to applaud and the rescued students and teachers followed suit, gradually rising to their feet as the Super Zeroes were led by the head of the Heroes' Alliance down from the stage and out through the central aisle.

Miss Flint turned to them as the doors to the auditorium

swung closed behind them all. "Well, you're on the side of the angels now, Mr. Cooper," she told Murph. "Here's your halo."

She handed him a slim phone handset, the same one that he'd seen Cowgirl use. The screen was blank except for the words HALO UNIT OPERATIONAL in small letters along the bottom. "This is the Heroes' Alliance Locator Unit. It's how you communicate with us," she told them, "but that's all you need to know for now. Keep it safe."

"How do I, you know, call you?" Murph asked Miss Flint in an undertone.

"You don't, Kid Normal," she replied. "We call you." And she turned on her heel and marched away.

26

The New House

All five of them danced out of school, chatting excitedly about what had just happened. They were actual superheroes! In fact, that's all they kept saying.

"We're actual superheroes!" whooped Billy.

"I know! We're actual superheroes!" replied Hilda.

"We. Are. ACTUALLY actual superheroes," confirmed Nellie.

But Murph wasn't being quite so vocal, because he'd spotted his mom waiting in her car outside the gates, and the realization that he was about to move once again came crashing into his brain. He had that sinking feeling you get when your parents come to pick you up from a party. You realize that the fun is over. He'd just pulled off the unimaginable, and how typical, he thought, that despite all he'd gone through, he'd have to start over again. In another new school that absolutely, one hundred percent, no question, would be nowhere near as amazing as this one. Why had he even taken the Heroes' Vow? He would never be able to live up to those words away from his friends.

Gloomily, he handed the HALO unit to Mary, mumbling, "You'd better look after this. Mom never wanted me to have a phone anyway." And he slouched across the road and slumped into the car, banging the door shut wearily.

Murph's mom had a few different faces that she used when picking him up from school, and he was an expert in them all. There was the "I've had a terrible day but I'm putting a brave face on it" face, the "let's go for pizza" face, the "tidy your room" face, and, worst of all, the "I'm not angry; I'm disappointed" face.

But today she was sporting an expression he hadn't seen before. It looked like she was practicing a new face—which you might call the "struggling to hold in a massive burp, but a good burp, a burp of excitement, not the burp you get after the aforementioned pizza" face.

As they drove, Murph was wondering why he wasn't being quizzed on the events of the last twenty-four hours. Why wasn't his mom saying anything? When he got into the car all she'd said was, "Ready?" and pulled away. When he started to ask about the house, all she did was hold up a finger for silence, still wearing her enigmatic burp face. Where were they going? They weren't heading the right way for the hotel.

Instead, they turned down a wide, tree-lined street and pulled up outside a house that can only be described as the exact opposite of the one he was living in until the previous afternoon when it was destroyed by a giant motorcycle-size robot wasp. Where the other house had been boxy and new, this one was interestingly shaped, with eaves and nooks and chimneys. Plus, it was old. Very old, in fact. It even had a well in the front yard, and that's how you know a house is really ancient. And underneath hanging ivy, the front door was painted blue. A good, solid, old-fashioned blue.

"Come on, then," his mom coaxed him. "Let's have a look inside."

Murph followed her in, wondering if this was the

house of some new friends she'd made or some sort of boring museum of bicycles. She'd taken him to one of those before, so he was on high alert. But there didn't seem to be anyone inside, or any bikes, thankfully.

Murph turned to his mom in the neat tiled hallway and asked the obvious question. "Who lives here, then?"

His mom looked like she was about to let out that brewing burp of excitement. "We do," she replied, raising her eyebrows.

"What?" replied Murph intelligently.

"WE DO!" she repeated, doing a mombarrassing dance of excitement.

"How?" said Murph, with a cautious grin appearing on his face. Even if it was only going to be a temporary place to stay until they moved, this was still going to be a pretty cool house to spend the summer in.

"The man from the insurance company sorted it out," said his mom, "and said he'd do all the paperwork for me and everything."

"O . . . kay . . . ," said Murph, immediately scenting outside interference. "What did he look like, this man from the insurance company?"

"Um, more like a soldier than anything else, I suppose," mused his mom. "He was dressed in black and wearing huge boots . . . Anyway, don't worry about all that. Go and have a look at your bedroom. It's right at the top. I thought you'd like the lookout tower so you can keep a watch on things!"

Murph zoomed up the stairs, past Andy, who was listening to music in his new bedroom through the world's biggest headphones. He darted up another set of stairs and pushed open the door.

Murph was stunned. What lay before him was his dream room. The beams of the roof made interesting sloping angles in the ceiling. At the front a wide skylight was open to the evening sky, and, best of all, at the back of the room, a wooden door led onto his very own balcony, which overlooked a long, overgrown, and winding garden.

He ran out and gazed over the roofs of the town glowing red in another rich sunset. This was the perfect base for the Super Zeroes. But before his imagination could run away with him, a familiar feeling of light dread descended upon him—as if a couple more baby eels had been set free in his insides. This new base would only be temporary, until he was snatched away from his friends once again.

He shook himself like a post-puddle wet dog and a few moments later bounded back downstairs. His mom was waiting for him with a cup of cocoa, looking like there was more of that excitement burp still to come.

Murph narrowed his eyes at her appraisingly. "What's up?" he said slowly, sensing mischief.

There was a smile about to burst out of her tightly clamped lips. They stayed glued together for a few seconds until they exploded open.

"We can stay!" she blurted out.

"WHAT?" Murph was stunned.

"My boss called me into his office first thing this morning and told me he'd found the money to keep my job open. We can stay. This is home. Our home. We're home!"

She grabbed her boy and gave him the biggest, most wonderful mom hug possible. One of those ones where everything bad is squeezed out of the world.

Murph noticed a flash of lightening over her shoulder. The other four Super Zeroes were gathered underneath the streetlight on the road at the end of their new driveway. Mary was skipping around and grinning while dangling a yellow mind-control helmet from one hand.

Murph broke off the hug. "Your boss . . . when he called you in," he began, "he didn't happen to be wearing any sort of hat, did he?"

"Yes, he was! How on earth do you know that? Some sort of weird yellow thing. I thought he'd just come in on his bike or something," she added. "But anyway, the contract's all signed!"

Murph and his mom looked each other straight in the eye. "That's great, Mom," he said simply, and they hugged again.

Looking over his mom's shoulder, Murph could still see Mary skipping around like an excited mongoose. His mom realized he was gazing out the window and craned her neck to have a look, too. Mary quickly hid the yellow helmet behind her back.

"Who are they?" said his mom.

"My friends," said Kid Normal proudly.

"Ah, the mysterious friends of yours! I was beginning to think they didn't exist," she replied, smiling a smile so big it nearly took up her whole face.

"Is it okay if I go and hang out with them?" he asked, knowing the answer.

"Of course," she said. "Go and have some fun." The last word came with a slight choking sound, along with another item from the ever-growing list of mombarrassments: proud tears.

Murph ducked out the door before it got too bad and darted toward his gang.

"What on earth have you been up to, Canary Girl or whatever it is you called yourself?" he asked, grinning from ear to ear.

"Rescuing you, silly. As per usual," Mary replied. "Welcome home. And since you are the leader of the Super Zeroes, I think you'll be wanting this." She was holding out the HALO unit.

Murph took the phone, which still bore the simple message **HALO UNIT OPERATIONAL**. He turned it over in his hands, wondering what he was supposed to do with it.

As if on cue, its bright green light began to flash. The message changed.

HALO ALERT. ALL UNITS RESPOND.

Murph looked up at his friends.

"Go on, then, answer it!" prompted Billy, one finger ballooning with excitement.

Murph lifted the handset to his mouth.

"Super Zeroes receiving!" he said firmly, recalling the words he'd heard the Posse use all those months ago. **"Kid Normal active."**

He was followed by the others.

"**Mary Canary active.**"

"**Balloon Boy active.**"

"**Equana active.**"

"**Rain Shadow active.**"

"**Alliance calling,**" said a calm voice from the phone. "**Attention, Super Zeroes. Please proceed as directed to—**"

But let's leave it there, shall we? I bet you'd love to know what the voice said next. And you will, in time. For now though, annoyingly, we're going back into the new old house for the final words of the book.

Here they come:

Inside the new old house, Murph's mom watched from the window, one mombarrassing tear still trickling down her cheek, as her youngest son and his new friends turned and dashed off into the gathering twilight.

THANKS ...

... first of all to our great friend, the wonderful Stephanie —the third member of Team Normal. Without you, Murph would still live in our heads.

Thanks also to the loveliest publishing people in the world at Bloomsbury, especially Hannah, who had to read this book five million times and still drew smiley faces in the margins beside the bits she liked.

Thanks to Erica for bringing the Super Zeroes to life. We love you, you inky-fingered Spanish genius.

Peace and love to Podcastards everywhere.

GREG WOULD ALSO LIKE TO SAY: To the special few people I invited into this world before it was ready, thank you for your love, support, and guidance. However, please don't tell Bloomsbury I did that because I'll get in trouble. And to Mum, Dad, and Sis, thank you for being my best mates and for making me realize anything is possible.

AND FROM CHRIS: They say the family of the 21st century is made up of friends, not relatives. Thanks to my entire family. And last but most, thank you Jenny for everything.

Without you it's a waste of time.

FINALLY: Thanks to **you**, for reading our story. Now go and write your own!

KID NORMAL

NORMAL

AND THE
SUPER ZEROES

WILL RETURN . . .

Don't miss their next high-flying, horse-summoning, storm-gathering, mind-blowing adventure!

KID NORMAL AND THE ROGUE HEROES

COMING JUNE 2019

GREG JAMES is a familiar voice and face on British radio and TV. He's the host of BBC Radio 1's award-winning show *Drivetime* and the *Official Chart* music broadcast. On screen, Greg has hosted a variety of shows, including the recent special BBC Children in Need, and in 2016 he raised over a million dollars for the charity Sport Relief by completing five triathlons in five cities in five days. He has no superpowers. In his spare time he enjoys the idea of having hobbies, but always tends to turn those hobbies into work.

CHRIS SMITH is an award-winning journalist and broadcaster who delivers the news to millions of people every day as the anchor of *Newsbeat* on BBC Radio 1. Chris enjoyed a previous glittering literary career as the winner of the H.E. Bates Short Story Competition in 1981 (under-ten category). Chris has no superpowers either, although he enjoys pretending his cat Mabel can fly by picking her up and running around.